We were dancing out there on the wet grass by ourselves, in the dark. I kissed her near the end of the song. She kissed me back.

I think we both felt changed, because we didn't smile or joke as we walked back toward the deck. You could cut the tension with a knife. It was sex. It was this great physical thirst that had come over us, and that we knew was coming, but weren't sure what to do with after its arrival.

"Kerr's first work since the highly acclaimed NIGHT KITES is part of a projected new series that will enthrall both her fans and new readers."

—*Publishers Weekly*

"Not since GENTLEHANDS has Kerr so poignantly combined a story of romance, mystery, and wit with serious implications of class conflict and personal betrayal."

—ALA *Booklist*

"Kerr's breezy style smacks with vitality and realistic humor."

—*School Library Journal*

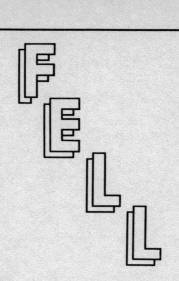

M.E. KERR Introduces

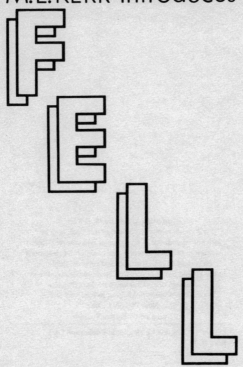

FELL

A Charlotte Zolotow Book

HarperKeypoint
An Imprint of HarperCollins*Publishers*

FELL

Copyright © 1987 by M. E. Kerr

All rights reserved. No part of this book may be
used or reproduced in any manner whatsoever without
written permission except in the case of brief quotations
embodied in critical articles and reviews. Printed in
the United States of America. For information address
HarperCollins Children's Books, a division
of HarperCollins Publishers, 10 East 53rd Street,
New York, NY 10022.

Designed by Bettina Rossner

Library of Congress Cataloging-in-Publication Data
Kerr, M. E.
    Fell.

    "A Charlotte Zolotow book."
    Summary: A strange incident on the night of the
senior prom changes John Fell's entire life, leading
him to enroll in an exclusive private school under an
assumed name.
    [1. Spies—Fiction. 2. Schools—Fiction] I. Title.
PZ7.K46825Fe   1987   [Fic]   86-45776
ISBN 0-06-023267-6
ISBN 0-06-023268-4 (lib. bdg.)
ISBN 0-06-447031-8 (pbk.)

Harper Keypoint is an imprint of Harper Trophy,
a division of HarperCollins Publishers.
First Harper Keypoint edition, 1988

BOOKS BY M. E. KERR

◻

Dinky Hocker Shoots Smack!
Best of the Best Books (YA) 1970–83 (ALA)
Best Children's Books of 1972, *School Library Journal*
ALA Notable Children's Books of 1972

If I Love You, Am I Trapped Forever?
Honor Book, *Book World* Children's Spring Book
Festival, 1973
Outstanding Children's Books of 1973, *The New York Times*

The Son of Someone Famous
(AN URSULA NORDSTROM BOOK)
Best Children's Books of 1974, *School Library Journal*
"Best of the Best" Children's Books, 1966–1978,
School Library Journal

Is That You, Miss Blue?
(AN URSULA NORDSTROM BOOK)
Outstanding Children's Books of 1975, *The New York Times*
ALA Notable Children's Books of 1975
Best Books for Young Adults, 1975 (ALA)

Love Is a Missing Person
(AN URSULA NORDSTROM BOOK)

I'll Love You When You're More Like Me
(AN URSULA NORDSTROM BOOK)
Best Children's Books of 1977, *School Library Journal*

Gentlehands
(AN URSULA NORDSTROM BOOK)
Best Books for Young Adults, 1978 (ALA)
ALA Notable Children's Books of 1978
Best Children's Books of 1978, *School Library Journal*
Winner, 1978 Christopher Award
Best Children's Books of 1978, *The New York Times*

Little Little
ALA Notable Children's Books of 1981
Best Books For Young Adults, 1981 (ALA)
Best Children's Books of 1981, *School Library Journal*
Winner, 1981 Golden Kite Award, Society of Children's
Book Writers

What I Really Think of You
(A CHARLOTTE ZOLOTOW BOOK)
Best Children's Books of 1982, *School Library Journal*

Me Me Me Me Me: Not a Novel
(A CHARLOTTE ZOLOTOW BOOK)
Best Books For Young Adults, 1983 (ALA)

Him *She Loves?*
(A CHARLOTTE ZOLOTOW BOOK)

I Stay Near You
(A CHARLOTTE ZOLOTOW BOOK)
Best Books For Young Adults, 1985 (ALA)

Night Kites
(A CHARLOTTE ZOLOTOW BOOK)
Best Books For Young Adults, 1986 (ALA)
Recommended Book for Reluctant YA Readers, 1987 (ALA)

Fell Back
(A CHARLOTTE ZOLOTOW BOOK)
1990 Edgar Allan Poe Award
Best Young Adult Mystery Finalist

FOR BOB MCKEON, WITH LOVE—TO REMEMBER BEGINNING DAYS
IN AUBURN, NEW YORK, AND EVEN BETTER DAYS IN
NEW YORK, NEW YORK!
AND
FOR ELEANOR APUZZO OF SOUTHAMPTON, NEW YORK, WITH
THANKS FOR THE LOAN OF GEORGETTE.

PART ONE

SMILES
WE LEFT BEHIND
US

ON THE NIGHT of the Senior Prom, I was stood up by Helen J. Keating—"Keats" they called her in Seaville, New York.

This isn't a story about Keats and me, and it isn't about that humiliating event in my seventeenth year. But Keats is a part of the story, and that humiliation was responsible for everything that happened to change my life . . . and even my name.

The Keatings lived on Dune Road, at the top of a hill in a palatial home. Adieu, they had named it, and it looked down on Seaville as surely as they did. It was the last house Keats's father would ever build—his good-bye to his profession. He was an architect of some renown, and certainly Adieu was an architect's dream. It was anyone's dream—who wouldn't like living in that place?

But to me Adieu meant good-bye in another way, from the moment I first saw Keats up there. It meant hello and good-bye. It meant good-bye, you can never have that girl. Say hello; then say adieu.

What does your father do? was the second question I was ever asked by Keats's father. The first one was How are you? Mr. Keating didn't wait for an answer. He didn't care how I was. He cared what my father did.

I said, "My father was a detective."

"Was?" he said. "Is he dead?"

"Yes, sir. He died six months ago."

"I'm sorry to hear that, Fell. That's your name, isn't it?"

"Yes. John Fell."

I would have liked to say (and Mr. Keating would have liked to hear me say), But, Mr. Keating, sir, I am heir to a fortune and descended from William the Conqueror, bound for Harvard University when I graduate from high school, a Christian, a Republican, an honor student.

If I could have said those things, he wouldn't have heard me anyway, for his plump behind was turned by then, and he was slapping his arm around Quint Blade, Keats's football star boyfriend. All of them up at Adieu that day would be seniors in the fall. I would be a junior.

I had been invited to that pool party by a fluke. I had waited on Keats in Plain and Fancy, the gourmet food shop where I had a part-time job. She'd wandered in there one afternoon after school to buy truffles with almonds in them, a quart of Häagen-Dazs coffee ice cream, and fresh everything from cherries to strawberries—a shopping bag filled with goodies and charged to her father's Diner's Club account.

"Aren't you the new boy at school?" she asked me.

"Sort of new. I've been here a year," I told her. But I *was* new to her and her crowd. I was new to any crowd in Seaville. (And the less said about my old crowd in Brooklyn, the better.) That was when she invited me to Adieu.

In between that party up at Adieu and her Senior Prom, we fell in love, blown away by the kind of passion that made Dante write about Beatrice, Tristram hunger for Isolde, and my father's last client dog the steps of his young, unfaithful wife, who sneaked off to road-houses where the jukebox roared and men drank beer from the neck of the bottle.

My father died sitting outside one of those places, waiting for something to report back to his anxious client. My father was always waiting outside someplace. A detective's life is not really filled with car chases and flying bullets. It is almost never what you see on TV. It is waiting with a thermos of coffee, and an extra pair of shoes in the backseat of your car, in case you're somewhere all day on your feet.

I had inherited his patience and his determination . . . and I would need them to be Helen J. Keating's lover. Love is never enough when there are parents whose dream for their only daughter does not include someone whose father had a heart attack in a 1977 Dodge Dart while waiting for a roundheels to leave a bar with someone she'd picked up inside. It does not include someone whose mother has gone over her $1000 limit on every charge card in her purse. (The morning of the Senior Prom, I'd found a Born to Shop decal in a store next to the florist, bought it, and attached it to the back of my mother's rusting white Volkswagen.)

Keats's mother we could handle. She was most famous in Seaville for her book reviews in *The Seaville Star*. She'd once reviewed a book called *Coke Is Not It!*, about kids who put themselves through college dealing drugs, with this lead paragraph: *If anyone's child is using pot or cocaine, I have yet to meet the parents, and I pride myself on getting out and about in my community. So who is to believe this author with her alarmist Henny-Penny warnings?*

That was Mrs. Keating . . . a tiny, smiling woman, suntanned in winter from visits to Palm Beach, forever warning Keats "Don't tell Daddy!" when she allowed us to go places and do things Mr. Keating would have denied us.

Once Mr. Keating got the idea that Keats and I were captured by a chemistry between us that compelled us to head for the dunes, or the game room in the basement of Adieu, or the backseat of the old Dodge I'd inherited from my father, he began to put his foot down. But Mr. Keating traveled as a consultant and a lecturer, and his foot was often miles away from Seaville, New York.

One day in late May we felt the full weight of that foot when he arrived unexpectedly at Adieu. Mrs. Keating was off at a Ladies' Village Improvement Society meeting, dealing with a way to prevent Dutch elm disease in the trees that lined Main Street. Keats and I were up in her yellow-and-white bedroom, listening to old tapes of Van Halen and Phil Collins, the rain pouring down outside. We'd just come from school, drenched, enough of our clothes drying over the backs of yellow chairs for Mr. Keating to see red.

"The Senior Prom is out of the question for you two!" Mr. Keating shouted. "Helen, the only way you'll get to it is to get yourself another date!"

It was Mrs. Keating who finally said, "All right! All right! All *right*! Go to the prom! I haven't the heart to say no! But don't tell Daddy!"

So with Daddy away, I went to Pittman Florist the day of the prom and ordered a white orchid sent to Keats. Across the card I wrote three words my father's last client had had embroidered across half a dozen silk nightgowns he'd given his young bride for a wedding gift: *Thine until death!*

When the box arrived at noon, Keats called me. "Oh, Fell! Thine until death! No one's ever written anything so romantic to me! I can't wait until tonight! Don't come at eight, come at five to."

"I'll be there at quarter to."

"No, come at twenty to."

We were always doing that, making our dates earlier and earlier, unable to wait.

I rented a white dinner jacket and black tuxedo pants. I bought a red boutonniere, and put a shine I could see my face in on a pair of my father's old black wing tips.

Maybe Keats and I were just narcissists, in love with

our own reflections. We looked enough alike to be brother and sister. Both of us had blond hair and deep blue eyes, though Keats claimed mine were really purple. She'd say, "I'm in love with a boy with purple eyes." Keats had shoulder-length hair, a long thin nose, and skinny long legs, and she always wore Obsession.

The rich don't live right on the road. They live up, back, and behind. From the time you enter the property at Adieu, you have a good three minutes before you see anything but trees. Once you see the house, you have another three minutes before you pull up to it. So on prom night I had six minutes to anticipate seeing Keats. Six minutes to gloat over the idea that I, a lowly junior, had beaten out Quint Blade in the contest for Keats. Six minutes to imagine my white orchid pinned to her, and that smile of hers that lights up rooms already aglow.

Now, looking back, I don't think anyone in Seaville, including my mother, ever thought Keats and I would make it through a year. We were a golden couple without a cheering section. No one was for us but us.

The Keatings didn't call Eaton a butler, but that's what he came off as, even though he doubled as caretaker. He wore an ordinary dark business suit when he answered the door.

"Good evening, Eaton!" I said jovially. Eaton could smile. I'd seen him smile. But he couldn't smile at me, or wouldn't, not even that night, when he must have known what I was walking into.

Foster, the black poodle, was sniffing my pants leg

as though I were a suspicious character. I'd never won the dog over, either.

"Mr. Fell," Eaton said, "Miss Keating left you this note and this package."

The note was one of those little white cards, folded over. Inside, her handwriting, with the circles over the i's:

Daddy came back right before dinner.
He's forcing me to go into New York City with him
and Mother. I tried to call you. I'm destroyed over it, Fell!
Thine until death, and after, and after that! K.

I looked up at Eaton, who had no expression.

I didn't want to have an expression, either, for him to take any satisfaction in, so I turned to go. I wondered if I could still walk now that my heart had fallen down into my shoes.

But Eaton was not finished.

"You have another message, Mr. Fell."

He handed me a small business card with raised print. On the front: *Lawrence O. Keating.* On the back, in a large, firm hand: *You are no longer welcome at Adieu! This ends it, Fell! L.O.K.*

Foster punctuated the message with an angry bark.

I went outside in a blur, clutching the small, gift-wrapped package. My father used to tell me never be ashamed of your tears, only be ashamed when you don't have any and the occasion calls for tears.

He would have been proud of me that night.

By the time I opened the gift from Keats—a purple silk bow tie—there were tears rolling down my face.

I shoved the tie back into its tissue and threw the box on the seat beside me. I took off with a lurch that kicked up the gravel in the driveway. I began to pick up speed as I headed down toward Dune Road.

Adieu is flanked by Beauregard on one side and Fernwood Manor on the other. All three driveways lead down to Dune Road.

The car I didn't see was coming from Fernwood Manor.

It was a dark-blue Mitsubishi I'd seen going in and out of there before. But I'd never come as close to it as I did that night—I rammed right into its back end. Then I sat there with my horn stuck, waiting for doom to descend.

That was how I met Woodrow Pingree.

2

ONE DAY KEATS and I watched them, through the elephant grass, on a dune out behind Adieu.

"Who are they?" I asked her.

"Woodrow and Fern Pingree," Keats said. "They live at Fernwood Manor. *Wood*row and *Fern*. *Fernwood*. Get it? Isn't that really gross, calling their house after their two first names?"

"At least it's in English," I said. "The Penningtons aren't French, and neither are you. So what's this Beauregard and Adieu? I think *that's* really gross."

"You just don't like Daddy," Keats laughed.

"Why didn't he just call it Good-bye? What's this Adieu crap?"

"Adieu sounds classier."

"It sounds more pretentious," I said.

She put her hand gently across my mouth and said, "Hush, Fell! Don't start in on Daddy. Let's watch the Pingrees instead."

Woodrow Pingree had the muscles of someone who

worked out regularly. From the neck down he looked like a man in his late thirties. Above the neck he was around fifty, white-haired, the cut close-cropped like someone in the military. He had a red hue to his face that my father's high blood pressure used to bring to his.

Woodrow Pingree was coming out of the water, even though it was a cold May afternoon, so chilly Keats and I were bundled up in sweaters. Fern Pingree was sitting back near the dunes, sketching.

"He's always going in in weather like this," said Keats. "I've never seen her go in, not even in summer."

"Is she drawing him, do you think?"

"I know she's not. She only paints the ocean. I saw an exhibit of hers at the Stiles Gallery. There are never any people in her ocean scenes, and get this!—she doesn't sign her name. She draws a teensy-weensy fern where the artist's name would be."

Fern Pingree looked much younger than Woodrow Pingree. When my father had that last client with the much younger wife, he'd tell me some men imagine that a new young wife will give them back their youth. I'd say, but what's in it for the new young wife? Money, usually, he'd say. He'd say those young women don't want to wait for a young man to make it, so they grab some old geezer who believes one of them when she says he's sexy, he's fascinating, he dresses too old for how she sees him. Oh, the crap they hand a poor guy you wouldn't believe!

Fern Pingree had inky black hair pulled back behind

her head. She was wearing white-framed dark glasses. She was dressed in a white jogging suit with a red down vest and a pair of those shiny olive Bean boots. She had her sketch pad propped up on her knees, but the moment she saw Woodrow Pingree coming toward her, she put it aside. She grabbed a white towel-cloth robe, got to her feet, and ran to meet him, reaching up to put the robe over his wet shoulders.

"His first wife died about eight years ago," said Keats. "That place never had a name until Fern came into his life."

"I don't think I'd name a place anything, either," I said.

"I don't think you'll have a place to name," said Keats. "What do chefs make a year? About twenty thousand?"

"I won't be just a chef. I'll own the place," I said.

"Oh, you'll *own* the place! Will the place be a Burger King, or a McDonald's?"

We were giving each other little pushes, clowning around until we heard Mr. Keating's voice bellowing out over the bullhorn.

"HELEN? I WANT YOU!"

"I want you, too, Helen," I said.

The first time old man Keating ever pulled that on us, we'd jumped as if someone were shooting at us. We'd been stretched out in the dunes and his voice had come booming over that thing like the wrath of God, ready to punish us for all we were about to do.

That afternoon, the Pingrees heard Mr. Keating's voice, too, and glanced up in our direction so that for a moment we were looking at them and they were looking at us.

"Damn Daddy!" Keats said, "That's really humiliating! I know he's watching us through binoculars, too."

"Let's give him something to look at!" I said, and I tried to grab her, but she pulled away. "I have to live with Daddy, Fell! You don't!"

I gave a little wave to the Pingrees as we stood up, but they didn't wave back.

"They don't encourage neighborly behavior," said Keats. "They don't even wave when they come out of their driveway the same time we come out of ours. Daddy says it's just as well. He doesn't want to know his neighbors, either."

"He knows the Penningtons."

"That's different. They're old money, and Skye Pennington is in my crowd. We don't know anything about the Pingrees."

I tried to take her hand, but she was thinking of Daddy with his binoculars out. The very thought of Daddy's watching us touch each other stopped Keats cold.

"We don't even know what Woodrow Pingree does for a living," said Keats.

"Ah!" I said, "The all-important question! What do you do for a living? What does your father do for a living?"

Keats let that one go by. "But they have this weird kid. He's not a kid, really, he's about your age." I was exactly one year younger than Keats, but in high school a senior is a senior and a junior is not a kid, really, he's about my age.

Keats said, "This kid goes to a military school down south somewhere. Daddy really hates him."

"He must have something admirable about him if Daddy hates him," I said.

"Last Thanksgiving Daddy was jogging down on the beach and this kid jumped out of the dunes and pointed a gun right at Daddy. When he pulled the trigger, a black balloon sailed out of the mouthpiece with BOOM! BOOM! written on it in white. Daddy almost had a heart attack before he saw that it wasn't a real gun. So Daddy called Woodrow Pingree, and do you know what that man said?"

"What?"

"He said, 'I'm sorry, but Ping loves tricks,' and then he laughed like it was funny."

"I think it's kind of funny myself."

Keats said what she always said, "You just don't like Daddy."

That was the only time I even thought about the Pingrees, until the night I drove into the back of their dark-blue Mitsubishi.

3

"YOU LOOK LIKE you're going someplace special," said Woodrow Pingree, after he lifted the hood of my Dodge and made the horn stop blowing.

"I was. I'm not now." I'd gotten out to face him.

He lit a Viceroy and shoved the little white Bic lighter back into the pocket of his sports coat. "This shouldn't take long. We just need to exchange some insurance information. You can probably still make it."

"I changed my mind," I said. "I'm not going where I was going."

He laughed as though I'd said something funny and told me he didn't think he was going where he was going, either.

"So follow me up to the house," he said. "We might as well be comfortable while we're writing down all the information."

I got back behind the wheel and waited for him to go up the driveway first. I had a melon-sized dent in my right front fender, but I figured I was ahead because he didn't seem at all angry about his back fender. At least this would help take my mind off Keats, who was probably a total wreck because she had to miss her Senior Prom. Things like that were important to Keats. She made a big deal over everything from Easter to Valentine's Day. She loved ceremonies, traditions, rituals . . . and the Senior Prom was a once-in-a-lifetime thing. It'd kill Keats not to show up there.

Fernwood Manor didn't look like much of a manor, not like Beauregard or Adieu. There were only two stories. It was built of stone and shingle, with only one chimney. There was a hedge out front, and some trees in tubs. There was a metal jockey holding out a steel ring.

Woodrow Pingree was smoking no hands as he got out of the Mitsubishi in the circular driveway. He took another look at the damage I'd done, then gave me as much of a smile as he could and still hold the Viceroy between his lips.

We started walking toward the front door.

"What's your name?" he asked me.

I told him. I told him that I knew his. I'd seen him go swimming one cold day in May.

"Was that you up there in the dunes? Were you with the Pennington girl or the Keating girl?"

"Helen Keating," I said.

"I tell my boy it's a shame. Two beautiful girls within walking distance and he won't even bother to go over and introduce himself."

He held the door open for me, and we walked down

this black-and-white tile floor, with a living room to the right, and a dining room the other way.

"Woody?" Mrs. Pingree was sitting on a white wicker chair in the center of the living room. She was an audience of one, facing this kid in a black top hat, who was standing behind a card table with a cloth covering it. He had on a black turtleneck sweater and black pants, and there was a black cape with a red lining over his shoulders. He had a wand in one hand. His glasses were about a half inch thick.

"It's all right, sweetheart! This young man ran into my car down at the bottom of the hill. Don't let me stop the show! We'll have a talk in my study."

He was sort of leaning into the room, without inviting me to go that way.

Mrs. Pingree had her white-framed dark glasses pushed back on her head. She was a tiny woman. I thought she looked a little like Yoko Ono, John Lennon's widow, without the oriental eyes. I guessed she was in her thirties.

"Then you're not going out, Woody?" she said.

"No, I'll be here."

He led me through the dining room toward another room.

"My son's going off to a summer camp for budding magicians in a few weeks," he said. "When he gets there, he has to put on a show. So he's practicing. Do you like magic?"

"Only sort of." I really didn't like it at all. I thought only real yo-yos did.

"I think my wife only sort of likes it, too, but she tries

to humor Ping. He's a nice boy, but he's like America was in 1491. No one discovered it yet." He chuckled at his own joke and led me into his study.

There were a lot of framed photographs lining the walls. There was a large desk, with French doors behind it leading out to a terrace.

He pointed to a leather armchair beside his desk and said to make myself comfortable. He said he was going to call "the Institute" and let them know he wasn't going to be there after all.

He punched out a number, then said to me, "I work at Brutt Institute in Bellhaven. Do you know the place?"

I shook my head no. I only knew that Bellhaven was down in Nassau County.

"No reason why you should," he said. "I'm a physicist. Do you like science?"

"It's my worst subject."

"Are you flunking it?"

"No, not flunking. But anything to do with science and I go down into the B's."

"So. You're mostly an A student," he said. And when I nodded, he added, "Like my son."

Someone answered the phone at that point. Pingree said, "Something's come up. I won't be by. No, nothing to worry about."

He put down the receiver. "I didn't have anything important scheduled. I've seen every one of my son's tricks again and again, so . . ." He let his voice trail off. "Did you bring in your insurance card?"

I got it out of the pocket of my white dinner jacket.

"After telling you to bring yours in I forgot to bring in mine," he said. "I'd better get it, so we can write down all the information. You want a Tab?"

"Do you have Coke?"

"Just Tab. My wife's always on a diet."

"Okay. Tab. Thanks."

He stood up. "You look like you were on your way to a dance. Are you sure you don't want to go?"

I told him my date got sick.

He stubbed out the cigarette he'd just lit and said he'd be right back.

I sat there for a while, glancing through a yearbook that was on the end of his desk. It was from The Valley Academy. The motto of The Valley Academy was *Ne Pas Subir*. Don't submit.

There were things written across photographs of boys in uniform.

Ping,
next time you make something disappear,
make sure it's you. Steve.

And,

I just told Brown
he was the most obnoxious boy in roll call,
but I'd forgotten about you, Pingree! George.

And,

Don't let me catch you in the dark,
if you come back next year, Nerdo! Al.

It was more of the same all through Woodrow Pingree, Jr.'s, yearbook. I wondered why any kid would bring it home to let his folks see. I wouldn't have.

I got up and walked to the French doors. I could see the lights of Adieu across the way. It seemed as though every light in the place was on. I wondered if Eaton was throwing a party over there while the Keatings were in New York City.

I opened the door to get more of a view just as Mr. Pingree returned with two Tabs on a tray, carrying his insurance card between his teeth.

I took the tray from his hands.

"That's a good idea," he said, nodding toward the terrace. "Let's sit out there."

After we went outside, he sat there writing out names and numbers he copied from our insurance cards. I stood, fascinated by the clear view of Adieu. Even the driveway lights were on. You could hear the ocean over the dunes.

Finally, Mr. Pingree tore a sheet of paper in half, handed me a piece of it, and said all the information I needed was there.

"I know now isn't a good time," he said, "but I'd like you to meet my boy sometime. He needs a buddy."

"I saw his yearbook in there," I said.

"He's through at Valley now. Are you a sophomore?"

"I'm going to be a senior."

"At Seaville High?"

"Probably not. My mother wants to move back to Brooklyn."

"So you're not from here?"

"No. Brooklyn."

"How long have you been out here?"

I told him, all the while staring over at Adieu. For someone who didn't even wave at his neighbors, he seemed really interested in a complete stranger. He asked a lot of questions. I found myself rattling on about my father's heart attack, my kid sister, my mother's job at Dressed to Kill—I even told him about the Born to Shop decal I'd stuck on the back of my mother's Volkswagen that morning.

He laughed hard at that.

I said, "I guess all women could use one of those decals for their bumpers."

"My first wife would have clobbered you for that remark," he said. "She was a feminist. She hated it when you tried to say females were this way or they were that way. She'd say that was sexist, and I'd say well, when the day comes when we don't know who's going to have the baby, the male or the female, we can stop talking about the differences between us."

I kind of liked him. But I couldn't give him my full attention, sit down and sip my Tab and shoot the bull with him, as he seemed to want me to do. I couldn't get Keats off my mind. I kept thinking of her on her way into New York City while her whole class was pouring out of cars right that minute, heading into the Seaville High gym, the band playing, all the girls wearing flowers.

"This dance you were going to, was it over at the high school?"

"The Senior Prom," I said.

He winced and said, "Ouch!"

"It's not so bad for me. It wasn't my prom. It was hers."

"The Keating girl's?"

"Yes."

"Still . . ." he said. "You wouldn't go stag?"

"I don't really hang out with any senior but her."

"Who do you hang out with? You have your own crowd?"

"I don't hang out that much."

"Oh. A loner. Like my son."

I said, "Well . . ." with a noncommittal shrug. I wasn't a loner, but the crowd I'd hung out with my last year in Brooklyn was filled with fast trackers. They were the kind my father'd take in off the streets and book, days he used to still walk a beat.

Pingree was a chain-smoker. He'd light one Viceroy after the other. He'd drop the spent butts into a seashell ashtray on the wrought-iron table in front of him.

He had very light sea-colored eyes. Around his neck he wore a scarf the same color, tucked into a white shirt.

I thought of the purple silk bow tie Keats had bought to match my eyes.

I watched Adieu.

"I didn't go to a high school," Pingree said. "I went to Gardner School. Did you ever hear of it?"

"No, sir." I was watching a car go up the driveway over at Adieu.

"It's a fine old school. My father went there and his

father before him. Now, Ping will enter there as a junior."

I knew the car. It was Quint Blade's silver Porsche.

"Pingrees have always gone to Gardner," said Woodrow Pingree.

Then I saw Keats.

I saw her walk out the front door of Adieu with Mr. Keating.

I watched Quint Blade get out of the Porsche and go around and open the passenger door for Keats. He had on a light-blue dinner jacket, with black tuxedo pants and a white ruffled shirt. Keats was in a long white gown, with gold slippers. She had a white cape over her shoulders. She had my white orchid.

"Those Gardner years were my happiest years," Mr. Pingree was saying.

I murmured, *"Ummm hmmm."*

"I still know all four verses to the school song," he said.

I had the feeling he was almost ready to sing them.

I watched Keats's father wave from the front steps as the silver Porsche pulled away.

I had to sit down or sink to my knees.

"Someday," said Pingree, "maybe I'll tell you about that school."

I figured he was this lonely man, with a young wife and a ditsy kid—a man who'd planned to drive down into another county to check in at his office just for something to do.

Then I came along. Someone to talk to—never mind

what I'd done to his Mitsubishi, this fellow needed someone to talk to.

When I visited my grandfather at his nursing home, he'd always try to get me to stay another hour. He'd say things like, "Someday I'll tell you what happened the first day your father ever walked a beat." William the Conqueror might not be in my background, but there were a lot of cops.

I'd ask my grandfather to tell me about it, and his eyes would light up. He'd say, "You want to hear about it *now*?"

But this man across from me was no relation. I couldn't rise to the occasion and do him any favors.

I kept thinking she'd called Quint Blade and he'd come running.

I swallowed my Tab, chug-a-lug.

"I have to go," I said.

"So soon?" Pingree said.

"So soon?" my grandfather would always say. "When is your father coming, Johnny?"

He's not, Granddad. He had a heart attack, remember?

Pingree got up when I did.

"I'll walk you out," he said.

4

THE TV WAS ON and my five-year-old sister was asleep on the rug in front of it, her paper doll and a bag of Chips Ahoy! beside her.

"Wake up, Jazzy," I said.

"Is it tomorrow?"

"No. It's still tonight."

"What are you doing home?"

"I got jilted."

"What's jilted?"

"Stood up. Keats went to the dance with someone else."

Jazzy sat up and rubbed her eyes. She checked to be sure the paper doll was there. She never made a move without the paper doll. She called the doll Georgette.

"Is Mommy home?" she said.

"No, Mommy doesn't seem to be home," I said. That teed me off, too. Our mother was supposed to be home by eight-thirty on Saturday nights. The store where she worked on Main Street closed at eight in the summer.

I'd felt bad enough leaving Jazzy alone at seven-thirty, when I'd left to go to Adieu. Mom said she'd be all right by herself for forty-five minutes. Mrs. Fiedler was right next door.

"I bet you didn't have any dinner," I said.

"Georgette had fwogs' legs," she said, caressing the doll.

"Say frogs," I said. "You're old enough now to say frog, not fwog." Then I leaned down and patted her blond curls, to make up for snapping at her. "I'll make you an omelet," I said.

"I don't want an omelet. I want your beef Borgan."

"My beef Bourguignon takes five hours to cook," I said. "I'll make you a cheese-and-tomato omelet."

"With bacon," Jazzy said.

"All right, with bacon. But it'll take longer."

I took off my white coat and undid my black silk tie.

"Can Georgette have your red rose, Johnny?" Jazzy asked.

"Tell her to help herself. I can't use it."

"Did you have a fight with Keats?"

"No, we didn't fight. Her father doesn't like me."

"I like you, Johnny."

"I know. I like you, too."

I went into the kitchen and started getting stuff out of the refrigerator.

Jazzy came in after me in a few minutes, carrying Georgette and the two shoeboxes that contained Georgette's wardrobe. Jazzy made all Georgette's clothes. In one shoebox the clothes were shabby: torn dresses, sweaters with holes in them, and tattered shorts and slacks. In the other shoebox there were short dresses, long dresses, hats, and fancy high-heeled shoes. Those clothes in that shoebox were trimmed with lace, decorated with real, tiny buttons, and colored with the brightest shades in Jazzy's crayon collection.

Jazzy's game was to have Georgette discover that her real parents were millionaires. She would dress Georgette in her poor clothes and serve her macaroni, or shredded wheat, or a few raisins. Then Georgette's real family would come by to claim her, and she'd be dressed in her other clothes and sit down to "fwogs'" legs or champagne and caviar.

When we lived in Brooklyn, my mother had a part-time job at The Gleeful Gourmet. She'd bring home some new delicacy for us to sample nearly every night: guacamole, cold lobster mousse, artichoke hearts with mushroom sauce—things we'd never tasted before. Sometimes my mother'd make salads for the place, or hors d'oeuvres or desserts, and I'd help her. That was when I discovered that I liked to cook, and that I was good at it.

My father'd retired from the force by then. He was doing private investigating. I'd fix him the food he'd take on stakeouts, surprise him with things like deviled meatballs, Chinese chicken wings, or stuffed grape leaves.

When we moved out to Seaville, after his first heart attack, we were talking seriously about opening a place like Plain and Fancy, where I'd gotten my part-time job.

What we hadn't counted on was the high rents for

stores in a resort area. The stores in Seaville cost from a thousand to two thousand a month.

Since my father's death, all Mom talked about was getting back to Brooklyn and opening something there.

I was just flipping the omelet over when my mother's Volkswagen pulled into the driveway, with the Born to Shop decal still fixed to the back fender. I figured she hadn't noticed it yet.

I told her that I'd been stood up, leaving out the encounter with Pingree because I didn't want to get her on my back about the dent in the Dodge just yet.

"Would you mind making one of those for me, too?" she asked. "I'm really beat! We had three customers come in at five minutes to eight. I said, 'We're closing at eight,' and one of them said, 'We won't be long.' What time is it now?"

"Quarter to ten," I said. "That's too long to leave Jazzy alone."

"Mrs. Fiedler was coming over every twenty minutes, Johnny."

"Mommy? Georgette had fwogs', frrr-ogs' legs for dinner!"

"That's nice, honey. I know it's too long to leave her, but I couldn't walk out on a thousand-dollar sale, and I called Mrs. Fiedler to be sure she was home and could check on Jazzy. A thousand dollars in an hour and a half, and only two of them were buying! I don't know where people get their money! Do they rob banks?"

"They put it all on credit cards," I said. "You know how that goes, Mom."

"Don't start on me tonight, Johnny!" she said. "Just because your fancy girlfriend stood you up, don't take it out on me!"

"Keats's father doesn't like Johnny," Jazzy said.

"Johnny should stick with his own kind if he doesn't want to be treated like a doormat," Mom said.

I passed Jazzy her omelet. "What's my own kind? Dad always said it was the wrong kind."

"It was! But that's over. We moved out here so you could meet just your average kind of kid. Can't you settle for your average kind? And now I hate it out here!"

"I hate it out here, too," Jazzy said.

"Jasmine, eat your omelet your brother was nice enough to make for you."

"Do you want cheese and bacon and tomato in your omelet, too?" I asked my mother.

"I'd eat ants and grasshoppers and spiders in my omelet at this point!"

Jazzy began to giggle.

Mom put her arms around her. "At least someone thinks I'm funny."

Mom did look tired, but she was still a good-looking woman, even after nine and a half hours behind the counter at Dressed to Kill. We were all blonds in our family, although my mother's hair was veering toward orange because of something she was using to "high-light" the color. My deep-blue eyes had come from my mother. Jazzy'd gotten her pug nose.

"How did your girlfriend get Quint Blade over there so fast?" My mother asked what I'd been asking myself ever since I left Fernwood Manor. "Don't tell me Quint Blade didn't have a date for his Senior Prom?"

"Maybe there are two jilted people with broken hearts tonight," I said. "Me, and Quint Blade's original date."

"Or just maybe she never intended to go with you at all!" my mother said.

"Mom, Keats was all excited this morning when the orchid arrived. She bought me a purple silk bow tie."

"I'd like to give her a purple fat lip!" my mother said.

"I'd like to give her a purple punch in the eye!" Jazzy said.

"Do you want your omelet firm or runny?" I asked.

"Runny," my mother said.

"Runny out the door and give Keats a purple kick in the pants," said Jazzy.

"Jazzy, *eat*!" my mother said. "So how did you find out that Quint Blade took Keats to the prom?" My mother sat with her elbows on the kitchen table, waiting for an answer.

I began to tell her about my run-in with Woodrow Pingree and somewhere near the end of the story, speak of the devil, the telephone rang.

"John Fell?" said Mr. Pingree. "What are you doing for dinner tomorrow night? Would you like to come here?"

5

SUNDAY MORNING I took Jazzy to St. Luke's, where she went to Sunday school and I went to church.

When we got back, Mom was standing in the kitchen, holding the phone's arm out with her left hand, muffling the receiver with her right. "It's Herself!" Mom said. "She's been calling you all morning."

We had our dinner at one o'clock on Sundays. I watched Mom pull a ham out of the oven while I spoke with Keats.

"I have to tell you something, Fell."

"I already know."

"How can you already know when you don't know what I'm going to say?"

"You're going to say you went to the prom with Quint Blade."

"God, I hate this town!" Keats said. "You can't even turn around in this town without everyone talking about it!"

"I'm going to be over your way tonight," I said. "Why

don't we arrange a secret meeting on the beach?"

Behind me, Mom said, "Don't let her treat you like some backdoor Johnny."

"What did your mother just say?" Keats asked.

"She said I was a backdoor Johnny."

"Oh, Fell! She's mad at me, too, I suppose."

"Why don't we meet clandestinely?" I asked. Keats once wrote a poem that began "Clandestine skies beckon me," which kicked off a long harangue from her English teacher, who said skies couldn't be clandestine.

"A clandestine meeting," she said, "under a clandestine sky. Shall we do something terribly clandestine?"

"Yes," I said.

"I'm glad you're not furious, Fell."

"I'm furious. I'm just holding it in."

"What do you mean you're going to be over my way?"

"I've got a date."

"You're stabbing me right through the heart, Fell. Last night wasn't my fault."

"Meet me down on the beach at nine o'clock."

Keats laughed. "That's not a very big date if you can get away by nine."

"Meet me down near Beauregard," I said.

"I love you, Fell."

"We'll talk about it."

When I hung up, Mom said she thought there was something fishy about that dinner invitation from Woodrow Pingree.

"I think he thinks I'll make a good companion for his son."

"What's wrong with his son that he needs a companion?"

"I think he's this loner or something."

"So are you. That's like the blind leading the blind," she said. "What's in it for you? Are you just going there so you can be within panting distance of Adieu?"

"No," I said. "I'm just curious."

"That killed the cat, and it killed your father, too."

"At least he was being paid for it."

"Paid to sit around, stand around, hang around—that was no life. Tell Jazzy she's to set the table. How was the new minister's sermon?"

"Jazzy?" I shouted into the living room. "Set the table! The new minister is one of those guys who makes you feel good about something you shouldn't feel good about," I said.

St. Luke's had just tossed out Reverend Shorr. In his place they'd hired Jack Klinger. He was a new, dynamic, Yuppie preacher who'd given a sermon the week before in favor of opening the North Shore Nuclear Plant, the one that a lot of people claimed wasn't safe to operate. He'd called his talk *Let Go, Let God!* He'd said faith was all about that: trusting. But I kept thinking, let go and meet God a few decades before you'd planned to.

This morning's sermon had been billed out front on the sermon board this way: *I Talk of Dreams/Shakespeare, Romeo and Juliet/Rev. J. J. Klinger, DD.*

"What did he make you feel good about that you shouldn't feel good about?" my mother asked.

"It wasn't me he made feel good. It was all the people

going to shrinks. All the people paying out a fortune to headshrinkers. Reverend Klinger said sometimes it's worth it."

"I'd like a headshrinker to help me figure out why we ever moved out here," said my mother.

"Reverend Klinger said shrinks help you discover what your dreams mean, the same way Daniel, in the Bible, helped Nebuchadnezzar find out what *his* dream meant."

"Never mind Nebuchadnezzar, why did I pick someplace to live where I can't make more than six dollars an hour?"

"*I* can tell you the answer to that," I said. "You don't need a shrink. You just didn't do any research on living in a resort area."

"Don't blame everything on me, Johnny. Your father wanted to make this move, too."

"You talked him into it," I said.

"Well, we're not going to stay."

"You keep saying that, but we never talk about how we're going to move back to Brooklyn, without an apartment to move into."

"Get Jazzy away from the TV and in here to set the table," my mother said.

She wasn't good at facing things, or making plans, until the last minute.

I was best at facing and planning clandestine meetings.

6

PINGREE'S SON ANSWERED THE DOOR.

He had these little pins for eyes behind thick swirls of glass, a kid about my age and height, with light-brown hair combed forward so that he looked as if he had bangs.

Without a hello or how are you, he pointed down at the black-and-white tile floor as I stepped inside. There was an ace of hearts there.

"I can change the face of that card," he announced.

I just looked at him. He had on a pair of faded blue jeans, a black tank top, a heavy military belt, and tan Top-Siders. My mother'd said, "Dress up when you go there for dinner. Don't always be locked into the Teen-age Look—they're probably fancy-schmancy." So I had on a dark suit, white shirt, and blue-and-white striped tie.

"With your permission?" he said.

"Okay." I shrugged.

He stepped on the card, took his foot away, and there was a five of spades.

I didn't know how he did it. The thing was, I didn't care. I didn't warm up to kids who said things like "with your permission?" I had as much curiosity about stunts like that as I had about Icelandic breakdancing.

He had this big, triumphant grin on his face. It reminded me somehow of Jazzy's smile when she was being toilet trained and could make it through a whole day without dumping in her Pampers.

I managed to mumble something congratulatory before I said, "I'm John Fell."

"Everyone calls me Ping."

"Everyone but my family calls me Fell."

His father appeared then. "All right, we'll call you Fell, too." He grabbed my hand in one of those viselike grips that's macho enough to knock your socks off. "Come into the living room, Fell!"

He had on the same sea-colored scarf that matched his eyes, tucked into another shirt as white as his brush-cut hair.

He stooped over to pick up the playing card.

"Ping? Hand over the other one, or you'll wonder where it went someday."

"You're not supposed to give away the trick, Dad."

"Oh, Fell could figure out that trick, easily."

I couldn't have. I watched while Ping lifted his left Top-Sider and bent over to take the ace of hearts off the bottom. So there'd been one card on top of the other. Ping'd fixed some adhesive to the bottom of his shoe, stepped on the ace of hearts, and left the five of spades there.

I hated having to be around anyone who made me feel sorry for him, or embarrassed by him. Right away I felt both ways about Woodrow Pingree, Jr.

We went into the living room and sat down. My mother would have called it "a tasteful room." It wasn't at all like any living room the Fells had ever occupied. In the Fells' living rooms you took your chances when you sat down. A pair of Jazzy's scissors or my mother's knitting needles could jab your butt. Our living rooms whispered clutter, clutter, clutter: old dog-eared magazines lying around under chairs, tabletops weighed down with books, soda cans, loose change, empty Lorna Doone boxes, crayons. We looked like an indoor yard sale.

The Pingrees' living room looked like something Macy's or Bloomingdale's had set up in its furniture department to show off its finest pieces. There wasn't anything out of place. There wasn't too much of anything in place. It was white and clean and modern.

"Is that gum off your shoes, Ping? Fern'll have your head if any of it gets on the rugs."

"It's off, Dad."

Ping removed his thick glasses and blew on them, then cleaned them with the bottom of his tank top.

I thought of a time way back in Brooklyn when my father'd found a pair of thick glasses smashed on the ground, beside the body of a man everyone thought had jumped out a window. My father'd said the minute he saw those glasses he'd known it wasn't a suicide. "Do you know why, Johnny?" I didn't. "Because," my father'd explained, "people who wear glasses and jump out of windows take their glasses off before they jump. They either leave them behind or put them in their pockets, but they don't ever jump with them on. So someone pushed that fellow."

Things like that interested me a lot more than magic tricks.

But I was in for an evening of magic tricks.

After Ping put his glasses back on he sat forward in an armchair and asked me, "What's half of twelve?"

"Six."

"Do you want me to prove it's seven?"

"It's up to you." That was as close as I could come to telling him I didn't know any way to stop him.

Apparently, Pingree didn't know how to stop him, either. Maybe Pingree didn't care that his kid was like some performing bear, compulsively going through his routine come hell or high water.

Pingree had returned the ace of hearts and the five of spades to a deck of playing cards. He was shuffling the cards quietly in his large hands, leaning back against the white couch, smoking. He was watching his son get out eight oven matches, which his son arranged on a table beside his chair.

Ping formed a Roman numeral twelve (XII), using four matches to make the X and four to make the II.

"Twelve. Right?" Ping looked over at me.

"Right."

Then Ping removed the four bottom matches, and what was left was VII.

Pingree said, "Bravo, son. Bravo."

There was more of the same before Mrs. Pingree called us into the dining room: card tricks, rope tricks, a handkerchief that turned into a rose, coin tricks, and the final trick, before we all sat down to a rib roast.

For this trick Ping borrowed his father's lit cigarette. There were four place cards made out of heavy paper, with nothing written on them, on the table.

"We have to see where everyone's sitting," said Ping.

He picked up the first card and touched the cigarette to it.

WOODROW PINGREE SR. burned itself out of the paper.

Then he made the rest of our names appear on the remaining place cards.

(Later, Mr. Pingree would let it slip that Ping had drawn out our names on the place cards with potassium nitrate. Again Ping would protest that it wasn't fair to give away "trade secrets.")

And so, we sat down to dinner.

Appearances are deceptive. My father used to tell me that that cliché, like so many others, was one you could rely on. What you know by looking at someone is zilch. I don't think I've learned that lesson yet. I certainly hadn't learned it by the time I went to Fernwood Manor for dinner.

There was something very different about Mrs. Pingree, other than the fact that she was a magician of sorts, too. Her talent was turning a prime cut of roast beef into leather. But it wasn't her cooking that interested me, beyond the first hard bite into the catastrophe she served with overdone asparagus and underdone new potatoes. It wasn't anything as simple as the fact that she could use a Julia Child cookbook.

"Skim milk masquerades as cream," I used to sing joyfully when I acted in Gilbert and Sullivan's *H.M.S. Pinafore* one year. It never dawned on me that cream could masquerade as skim milk just as easily.

Fern Pingree had a way of being present without being there—not so you'd notice, anyway. She behaved as though her purpose was to serve us, listen to us, and not watch us. She watched what was in front of her. She sat with lowered eyes, her very black hair held back behind her head with a piece of white net tied in a bow. She had olive skin, small hands, and a gentle, whispering voice. She seemed to be some female from another country, an Eastern one, where females did not participate equally with men.

No one tried to draw her into the conversation.

Second only to being with someone who makes you feel sorry for him or embarrassed by him, I hated being in a group with someone who was ignored. No one directed any conversation to her, or sought out her eyes, or even glanced her way.

The conversation began with some questions directed at me by Mr. Pingree. The usual. What subjects I liked in school, family stuff, how we'd come to live in Seaville . . . and I threw Keats's name in a couple of times. I didn't have the heart to mention that I loved to cook, not with what was on the plate in front of me.

Mrs. Pingree didn't ask me anything. She seemed to be part of the conspiracy to keep her out of things. I couldn't be sure if she preferred it that way, or just deferred to the male Pingrees.

I waited for her to say something about the dinner, the way my mother would have—"Oh, *no*, I think I overdid the roast!"—some little acknowledgment that she knew what we were eating wasn't wonderful. . . . Nothing.

Now and then I'd get a whiff of this sweet gardenia scent coming from her, almost as if to remind me she was still there. There was little else to remind me. I caught occasional glimpses of her out of the corner of my eye.

The conversation turned to a dream that Ping kept having.

Like the yearbook from The Valley Academy, which I wouldn't have brought home, with all the bummers written across the other cadets' faces, the conversation was one I wouldn't have had with my father, not in front of a guest.

When Ping told the dream he put down his fork and gestured with these stubby fingers. "There are stairs going up to a tower. I don't want to go up them." He glanced at me. "I have a fear of heights, Fell! I have a phobia about heights!"

His father was looking down at his dinner, chewing,

holding both a fork and a knife while he ate.

Ping continued. "But I must go up those stairs. Halfway up, a jack-in-the box pops out at me and hands me a card. D.D.H. are the initials on it."

"What's that supposed to mean?" Pingree asked.

"I'll tell you! I turn the card over, and written there is *Don't. Dare. Hope!*"

Ping leaned toward his father. "You see, the tower is the one at Gardner School. I don't want to go up in it. The jack-in-the box is telling me not to hope that I won't have to. The dream is about my not wanting to go to Gardner, Dad!"

There was a long silence.

I can't stand a silence like that. I'll start to babble about anything to fill it.

What I said was, "At church this morning, the minister preached a sermon on dreams. He said shrinks are as good as Daniel was at helping Nebuchadnezzar figure out what his dream meant."

"I know what mine means," Ping said. "And so does Dad."

That was when Fern Pingree finally spoke up.

"Dreams don't have meanings!" she said flatly. She was looking up now, meeting all of our eyes as she continued. "Dreams are just mental noise. They're neurological junk the brain is discarding. Dreams are the trash bag of the brain!"

I never expected anything like that to come out of her mouth.

"I don't happen to believe that, Fern," said Ping.

"It doesn't matter what you happen to believe. Those are the facts!"

"Why does the dream come again and again, if it's just junk the brain's getting rid of? Why the same dream again and again?"

"Because," said Mrs. Pingree, "recurring dreams are those that wake the dreamer and cause him to learn instead of unlearn them. A recurring dream is a kind of neurological flypaper."

"Well, Freud would say you were wrong, Fern," Ping said.

"Not if Freud were still alive. A lot has been learned about the brain since Freud was around."

"You always have an answer for everything," Ping said sullenly.

Mr. Pingree said, "And we always have a solution." He did something I thought was peculiar then. He put down his knife and fork long enough to reach across and grip Ping's arm. "We always have a solution," he repeated.

Mrs. Pingree, in a white cotton jumpsuit, stood up and got the salad from across the room. "Do you like salad on that plate or a separate plate, Fell?" she asked me, and without waiting for an answer, added, "Daniel tricked Nebuchadnezzar, Fell. He wanted power over the Babylonians!"

I didn't have an answer to that.

"I'll take the salad on this plate," I said.

She stood in front of an enormous oil painting on the wall. It was the most barren landscape I'd ever seen.

There wasn't anyone in the picture. It was a painting of this field of weeds on dried earth, with an abandoned barracks far off in it, weathered and worn. Above everything was this burning yellow sun that looked hot enough to make an iguana pant. At the bottom left was a parched white cow's skull. At the bottom right, a minuscule fern where the signature of the painter would have been.

"Isn't that one of your paintings, Mrs. Pingree?" I asked her.

"One of my early ones," she replied. "I did it long before I started at the Institute. Since I've been at Brutt, I've only painted the ocean."

She glanced over her shoulder at her strange landscape.

She said, "I call that one *Smiles We Left Behind Us*."

That was just spacey enough for me to grin, but Mrs. Pingree wasn't smiling.

No one was.

"I didn't know you worked at the Institute, too," I said. "What do you do there?"

Mr. Pingree said, "She's my boss, Fell."

回

It was Mr. Pingree who walked me down to my car after dinner.

"My son doesn't want to go to Gardner," he said.

I wondered why he thought I gave a damn what his son wanted, and why I'd even been asked to Fernwood Manor for dinner in the first place.

"Anyone would give his right arm to go to Gardner," he continued. "It's a wonderful school! But it's in Pennsylvania, this little town filled with ragweed, hell on Ping's asthma, and then there's The Tower. A very tall one. New boys are made to go up in it. My son has a phobia about heights, as he mentioned."

I was already imagining how Keats and I would make up. We wouldn't stay down on the beach, not with me in my dark suit, and not in the cold night air that was beginning to blow off the sea.

No. I'd park my car behind Beauregard. We'd go there to make up. Keats and I had nicknamed the backseat of my Dodge "The Magnet."

Pingree said, "If you had the chance to go away to an excellent prep school, wouldn't you jump at it, Fell?"

"I suppose so."

"Of course you would. But Ping has his reasons. They're valid."

We stood by my Dodge.

Pingree said, "Come back, won't you, Fell?"

"Thanks," I said.

Thanks wasn't yes.

There was a moon rising with the wind and I thought of the way Keats sometimes touched my lips with her fingers, smiling promises.

D.D.H., I laughed as I got into the Dodge and drove away from Fernwood Manor.

KEATS HAD THE KIND OF FACE that told you right away what her mood was, and that night in the moonlight it said down.

"What's the matter?" I said.

"Mother's reviewing this book by this poet named Lorine Niedecker, and I read one of her poems and I feel awful, Fell."

"Well, get over it," I said. "It's just a poem."

"You know what she wrote? She wrote, *Time is white, mosquitoes bite, I've spent my life on nothing*," Keats said. "That's exactly how I feel, Fell."

"You haven't spent your life yet."

"I've spent eighteen years of it. On nothing."

"Thanks," I said.

"I didn't say on no one. I said on nothing. I'm going to be this terrible failure, Fell. I can feel it in my bones."

We started walking along the wet sand, Keats barefoot with her jeans rolled up, a cold wind coming off the ocean that made me shiver. Keats just had a sweatshirt on. She was never cold, even in winter in below-zero weather. I always was.

"You have to *try* something first, before you can be a failure," I said. "One step at a time."

"I don't even know what to try. I want to *be* someone, but I know I'll end up like Lorine Niedecker."

"At least she's published."

"She's dead, Fell. And no one ever heard of her but my mother and some other reviewers who got the book free in the mail, so they'd write something about it."

"Keats," I said, "I didn't come down here to talk about Lorine Niedecker. How did Quint Blade get over to your house so fast last night? Why did you lie in your note?"

Silence, except for the sound of the waves hitting the beach and a plane passing above us among the stars.

"Well?" I said.

"I don't like myself for any of that," said Keats. "If I liked myself for doing something like that I'd have made it more foolproof. You found me out right away. I probably wanted to be found out."

"You didn't want to be found out," I said. "So don't make it into something deep. I probably wouldn't have known if I hadn't run into your neighbor's car last night."

I told her about it. I told her how I'd seen her get into the silver Porsche from the terrace of Fernwood Manor.

"I would rather be anyone but me, Fell," she said. "Daddy didn't come home last night. He got home the night before."

"Great!"

"He'd come out on the jitney with Quint Blade. Quint

told him Tracy Corrigan had come down with the flu and he didn't have a prom date. So Daddy said . . .''

I cut her off. "Daddy said, 'Why, you can take my daughter. My daughter will be happy to stand Fell up.' ''

"No, that's not what Daddy said and you know it! Daddy didn't even know we had a date! I couldn't get Mother in hot water by telling him we had a date, could I? So Daddy just told Quint to call me, and Quint called me.''

"You knew you weren't going with me when you called to thank me for the orchid," I said.

"I wanted you to be happy for as long as you could, Fell.''

"Then out, out, brief candle."

"Something like that. Only I kept you lit all day, right up to the last minute.''

I slipped my arm around her waist. "You're not spending your life on nothing. You're spending it on deceit and manipulation.''

"I don't *like* it.''

"I don't much like it, either.''

"I didn't have a good time at the prom.''

"Tell the truth," I said.

"It wasn't a rotten evening or anything like that, but I missed you, Fell.''

"Well, at least my white orchid got to the prom.''

"It wasn't yours once you sent it to me. You always do that, Fell. You call my gold bracelet your gold bracelet, and you call the ring you gave me your ring.''

"Sorry," I said. We walked along with the ocean spray

hitting our faces. "How come *I'm* the one saying I'm sorry tonight?"

"I'm sorry, too," Keats said. "Quint had four teensy little brown orchids on a branch for my wrist, but I hate wrist corsages! I decided to wear the white orchid."

"You have a hard life, Keats," I said. "Decision after decision to make."

"Don't. I'm really down," she said. "Daddy hates you."

"Well, I don't exactly love Daddy, either."

"I think he's going to send me to tennis camp, Fell."

"What do you mean he's going to *send* you to tennis camp? You're not ten years old! He can't send you somewhere you don't want to go."

"That's just it," said Keats. "I do want to go."

"This could be our last summer!" I said. "Do you want to spend our last summer in tennis camp?"

"Daddy says he doesn't want me to see you, anyway."

"So we'll sneak around."

"I don't want to spend the whole summer before I go away to college sneaking around!"

"Keats," I said, "I'm cold."

"Where's your car?"

"In back of Beauregard."

"I'm afraid if we get into The Magnet we'll just fight."

"We won't fight," I said.

"We'll just start talking about everything and fight."

"We won't talk about everything."

"Do you promise?"

"I promise."

"What will we talk about if we don't start talking about all this?"

"We won't talk."

I was turning her around, and she was almost following.

She stopped. "What will we talk about on the way?"

"The Pingrees," I said.

"Oh, hey," she said, "I forgot to tell you something." She was going with me back toward Beauregard then. "Mr. Pingree actually spoke to Daddy today, right down here . . . and it was about you, Fell."

"What do you mean?"

"Out of the blue," Keats said. "Daddy was down here letting Foster run, and Mr. Pingree said hello, and then Mr. Pingree said he was thinking of hiring you and he wondered what Daddy thought of you."

"Hiring me for what?"

"He didn't say. He just said he knew you dated me and he wondered what Daddy thought of you."

"So what did Daddy say?"

"Daddy would never blacken your name, you know that. Daddy's always said you might be right for some other girl, you're just not right for me."

"So what did Daddy say?"

"Daddy said we used to date, but we don't date anymore. See? We're starting to talk about it."

"No, we're not starting to talk about it! What else did Daddy tell Pingree?"

"Daddy just said you'd probably be a good worker.

That's all. Daddy said we weren't dating anymore and you'd probably be a good worker. He said the conversation didn't last two minutes."

"I wish you'd told me this!"

"How could I tell you? It only happened this afternoon."

"Why didn't you tell me a few minutes ago, when I told you about running into Pingree's Mitsubishi?"

"It slipped my mind, Fell! I'm depressed tonight! I don't have any real goals!"

"Never mind all that!" I said. "Don't start in on all that again!"

"What does Mr. Pingree want you to do, Fell?"

"It beats me!"

"I think that's why Daddy just suggested tennis camp. He doesn't want me around with you working right next door."

"I *have* a job," I said, "at Plain and Fancy."

"Then what does Woodrow Pingree want to hire you for?" Keats asked.

"It's the first time I heard about it," I said.

"Didn't he mention it at dinner?"

"No. Maybe he changed his mind."

"Maybe you picked up the wrong fork or something." Keats bumped against me playfully, more like her other self.

I laughed. "I guess he got turned off when I drank out of my finger bowl."

"You know what Daddy said?" Keats asked. "Promise not to get mad?"

I put my thumbs in the corners of my mouth, screwed my features into a monster face, and said, "Do I look mad, my girl?"

"Daddy said maybe their cook quit."

"Oh, Daddy's a riot!" I said.

"I knew you'd get mad."

"For Daddy's information, there are chefs, there are restaurant *owners* who make just as much as Daddy ever made!"

"See? We're doing it, Fell," Keats said. "That's what I mean. We can't stop talking about it all!"

"Yes, we can!" I said. "C'mon!" I grabbed her hand and we began to run until the lights from Adieu and Fernwood Manor were back in the distance.

AT THE END OF JUNE, Keats went off to Four Winds, a tennis camp in Connecticut. She said we could do our sneaking around up there, and some weekends I drove up to Greenwich and we did.

Four Winds also had a theater program. Keats couldn't resist any kind of dramatics, whether they were her own or Tennessee Williams's.

"You've got to come up a week from next Saturday," she said. "I'm going to be in *Cat on a Hot Tin Roof*."

"I'd rather come on a weekend you're not in a show," I said. "You're too hyper at showtime."

"I'm only in this damn thing to impress *you*, Fell!"

I was getting the eye from Keith Cadman, the owner of Plain and Fancy. It was a Friday, late in the afternoon, and the weekend animals were arriving in their Audis and BMWs. The line at the cheese counter was all the way up to desserts.

"I'll be there," I said. "I'm already impressed, though, or didn't you notice?"

"I noticed, but I can't get enough. I'm insecure. Speaking of which, I had a terrible dream that you were dating Skye Pennington, and I could see you through Daddy's binoculars in her bedroom at Beauregard."

"Dreams are just mental noise," I said. "They're neurological junk the brain is discarding."

"FELL!" Cadman yelled. "Get back on the floor!"

"I need my ego boosted, Fell," said Keats.

"I specialize in boosts to the id," I said.

"Because you're a dirty-minded high school boy," she said, "getting your kicks with an older woman. Hurry, Fell! I need any kind of boost you can give me! I miss you!"

"Miss you, too," I said.

I hustled back to the floor to wrestle with the wheels of brie and the crocks of goat cheese. I was trying to look at my watch without Cadman seeing me do it. He was already p.o.'d with me for baking a couple of their famous White Raisin Dream cakes and forgetting the raisins. I'd frosted them and renamed them "Remembering Helen," in Keats's honor.

"What the hell does that mean?" he barked at me when he showed up that noon. "First you leave out the raisins, then you stick that pink guck on them and name them *that*!"

But they'd been selling all morning and were almost gone by the time Cadman was simmering down.

"People like kinky names on things," I told him.

"I'm running this place, Fell."

"If we renamed the Black Walnut cake something like

'Smiles We Left Behind Us,' we'd sell that out, too."

"We're not in show biz here, Fell."

The Pingrees were still on my mind, way into July. I wondered if I'd ever know what Woodrow Pingree had wanted from me that night in June. I doubted it. I suspected that it had to do with Ping. I figured that he'd changed his mind when he'd noticed that magic tricks didn't really thrill me.

I sold a lot of brie and a lot of blue cheese dip, all the while looking forward to a date I might have that night. I wasn't dating Skye Pennington, but I was going to try dating. Keats was, too—I'd bet anything on it. Four Winds was coed. I knew Keats. She was up to something at that place on weekends I wasn't there. Neither one of us formed our A-one relationships with the same sex.

My "maybe" date that night was with a summer girl named Delia Tremble. She was always coming into Plain and Fancy to buy the latest fads for the woman she worked for: fiddlehead ferns, or sun-dried tomatoes, or green peppercorns. She'd always wait for me to help her: pitch-black hair spilling down her back, dark eyes, a sexy body—Tremble was right. I'd go up to her and she'd start grinning and looking all over my face while she talked to me. She said she was hired to take care of these twin kids who were always with her.

After about ten days of convincing myself I needed a dark lady in my life, I asked her if she liked going to movies. She said no, they had a VCR where she worked, but she liked to dance outdoors. I told her I knew where they did that, and she said if she could get off that Friday she'd like to go. I was going to call her at nine-thirty, after she got the kids to bed.

She gave me the address where I could pick her up. It was an address south of Montauk Highway, meaning it was near the ocean, like Adieu was—and Beauregard, and Fernwood Manor.

My mother said, "Aren't you ever going to get out of that neighborhood? Maybe you should get a job in K-Mart so you can meet your own kind."

"She's my kind," I said. "She's just an au pair there. She's your average person you're always talking about."

"Don't get too attached to her," Mom said. "We're not staying out here."

It was the summer of my discontent, as Shakespeare put it once about Richard the Third's winter. Keats was away doing God knows what besides playing tennis and acting in plays. Even if I got really turned on by Delia Tremble, she'd said she lived in New Jersey . . . a long way from Seaville, or Brooklyn. Fall was right around the corner, and where would I be then?

Lately Mom was saying your fate is already set; you just lean into it. The Mysterious Mr. X had told her that. He was this customer who came into Dressed to Kill, bought things like ninety-dollar pants in about two minutes, didn't even try them on, then stayed to chat with Mom for an hour at a time.

"Is he flirting with you?" I asked her.

"If he is," she said, "he's a glutton for punishment, because all I ever talk about is you and Dad and Jazzy."

At about two minutes to six, Cadman rang the chimes that meant everyone out. I began to undo my apron strings. I was planning to use my employees' discount to get a Droste Dark Chocolate Apple for Delia Tremble. I walked up toward the candy and heard a voice call, "Fell!"

He was standing by the coffee grinder, holding a bag of French Roast beans. He had on yellow linen pants, that scarf he seemed to love, a yellow cotton shirt, and rope sandals. He was smoking, even though there were No Smoking signs up. After I said hello, I started to take the package from his hands to pour into the grinder.

"No, thanks, Fell," Mr. Pingree said. "We have a Toshiba at home that does that. . . . How are you fixed for dinner?"

"I usually just go home. I might have a date later, too."

"I'm going to take a drive out to Lunch now, for some steamers. Does that interest you?"

Lunch was a place on Montauk Highway, just outside of Amagansett. It was a ten-minute drive. They had the best of everything there, from fish and chips to home-made pies and cakes. It was just a little shack, nowhere you'd spend a long time at, and you didn't need to be dressed up. You could sit outside and eat, too.

I hadn't had steamers yet all season.

Pingree said, "Ping's in camp and Fern's in New York City."

That clinched it for me. I said, "Why not?"

When I called Mom to tell her, she said, "Aren't you supposed to call your new girlfriend tonight for a date?"

"Mom, I'm old enough to keep track of my own calendar."

"Well, excuse me!" She said it the way the comedian Steve Martin used to say, "Well, excuuuuuuse *me!*"

"I'll be home later to change my clothes, anyway," I said.

"Good, because I have a surprise for you. I opened a charge account at Westway today."

"Oh, Mom."

"Don't oh, Mom, me. We need some things. They had a sale on corn poppers. I got one, and I got a Micro-Go-Round, a Little Leaguer top for Jazzy, and something for you."

"To wear?" I asked, hoping the answer was no.

"To wear on your date, if you have one."

I didn't like her to buy me clothes. She'd get me stuff like a "spring knit top" made in Korea. I'd wash it a few times and it'd tear if I opened an envelope while I was wearing it.

I told her I'd see her later, and to be sure the Mysterious Mr. X was out of the bedroom by then. She said, "That ends my ever telling you a single thing about my customers! Your mind is warped!"

"Did you get your dent fixed, Fell?" Pingree asked me as we went out to his Mitsubishi. I said I had. I could see his dent was still there.

He said, "I reported it but I haven't had time to take it in and leave it there. I've been away. I drove Ping to Tannen's—that's the camp for kids who are budding magicians. Then I flew out to Las Vegas for a while. You see, I like cards, too, but I like to play cards, not do tricks with them."

"I don't like either very much," I said.

We got into the Mitsubishi. "What *do* you like, Fell?"

"I like to cook. Someday I'd like to own a restaurant."

"That takes money."

"Yeah, that takes money."

"Well, don't sound so discouraged. There are ways to get money."

I watched him light a cigarette and thought about his saying "get" instead of "make." Just listen carefully, my father used to say, and people will tell you all they don't want you to know about themselves.

"At least you weren't born rich, Fell," said Pingree.

"For sure."

"You're ahead of the game if you weren't born rich," he said. "We had a certain amount of money when I was a boy. Then we lost it. It's harder to get over something like that than it is to get over being poor."

"I suppose that's true."

"It is, Fell. Most of your big entrepreneurs never had a dime. That's what drove them. But people like me—

we grew up with the mistaken idea that we're entitled to it."

"I see what you mean."

"You see what I mean, Fell? Then we get sent off to someplace like Gardner."

Back on that, I thought.

All roads lead to Gardner.

"YOU SEE, Ping's in an unusual and enviable position," Mr. Pingree said. "He'll actually get paid to go to Gardner."

I was pigging out on the steamers. There wasn't a speck of sand in them. They were little and juicy, and the butter was real butter and warm.

"Who pays him?" I said. I ate the tails, too. Keats said you weren't supposed to eat the tails, and it was really gross to see someone do it, but I always ate them. Once Keats said what do they taste like? They couldn't be good. I told her they tasted like rubber erasers at the ends of pencils. They tasted like good rubber erasers at the ends of pencils.

Pingree said, "Ping's grandfather left twenty thousand in his will. Ten thousand goes to Ping when he finishes his junior year at Gardner. The other ten is his when he graduates."

"Neat!" I said.

Mom hired this kid to take my grandfather out of the

nursing home one afternoon a week, to get him a good meal in a luncheonette called Little Joe's. They made things like macaroni and cheese, meat loaf, franks and beans—it was a mom-and-pop place near Carroll Gardens in Brooklyn. This kid would sit across from my grandfather and let him talk while the kid ate as if there were no tomorrow. I felt like that kid.

"Ping isn't impressed with money," Pingree continued. "Two things that always kept my wheels oiled don't even make Ping's spin: love and money. He hasn't any interest in either."

Out in the parking lot near the dunes, gulls were circling overhead, waiting for customers to toss out corners of clam rolls, or potato chips.

"Money and love," Pingree said. "They'll both make you and they'll both break you."

"For sure," I said.

"You at your age," Pingree snickered, "you can't even see the tip of the iceberg yet."

I tore off some bread from a thick slice, to soak up some of the clam juice left in the shells.

Pingree said, "The person you think you'll love all your life when you're your age, when you're my age you'll either feel sorry for, or trapped by, or bitter over, if you marry her. Possibly all three. I married my high school sweetheart, only I was in prep school, of course, and she went to boarding school."

I got a fresh napkin out of the metal container on the table, and wadded up the old, wet one.

"After Ping's mother died," Pingree went on, "I married my Fern. I think poor Ping suffered because I loved her so much. He was little, getting over his mother's death still, and I'd fallen for Fern like someone your age falls. I was besotted. Do you know that word?" He didn't wait for my answer. "That's a good word," he said. "Besotted . . . I owe Ping something for that. Do you want more butter?"

"Sure. Thanks."

He signaled to the waitress, pointing at the small green dish between us with a quarter inch of melted butter in it.

He wasn't eating much. My grandfather'd eat like a bird at Little Joe's, but the kid who took him there ate a couple of entrees and a couple of desserts. He never said anything.

My grandfather'd complain, "That kid sits like a dummy, like a dummy who's been starved." I didn't like feeling like the starved dummy.

So I spoke up.

"If you could have love or money, but not both, which would you rather have, Mr. Pingree?"

"You can call me Woody."

I wasn't so sure I could. He was a lot older than my father'd been when he died. He was older than most of my teachers at school.

"That's a good question, Fell," he said.

It was a fantastic July evening, white clouds floating around in the sky like big pillows. We were sitting on the outside porch, under a red-and-white-striped awning. You could hear the ocean just over the dunes.

Pingree said, "I'd choose love if I could trust it. I'd choose money if I could hang on to it."

"But which?"

He thought about it. I'll give him that. He frowned and passed one hand over his white hair, looking up from his clams.

"If I have to choose, I'll choose money," he finally said. "I understand it better, and I need it more."

There were a couple of kids racing by, waiting for their parents to finish eating, and their mothers were screaming at them, "Don't run!"

"I'm going to tell you something, Fell, and it may shock you."

What shocked me was what I saw driving into the parking lot: a battered white Volkswagen with a Born to Shop decal on the rear bumper.

I didn't believe it, but there they were. Mom must have left the house about two minutes after I'd mentioned steamers on the phone. That was probably all she needed to hear to start her mouth watering.

The Fells were seafood lovers. Summer nights back in Brooklyn we'd pile into the Dodge and drive out to Lundy's for the Shore Dinner at the drop of a hat.

I looked back at Pingree. He'd put down his clam fork to light a cigarette.

"You were about to shock me," I said.

He took a drag on the cigarette. He said, "My son hates Fern no matter how she tries to please him. He thinks she was responsible for his mother's death. You see, we all worked at the Institute together: Ping's mother, Fern, and I. We were all close friends."

"What *is* the Institute, Mr. Pingree? What kind of work do you do there?"

He shrugged. "Research, mostly. For the government. Classified, so it rarely gets publicized. I think that disappoints Fern, too. She's blooming in a bowl. But that's another story."

"How did Ping's mother die?" I didn't have any choice but to call her that. Pingree couldn't seem to say her name.

"It was a boating accident. Ping's mother knew boats. Fern didn't. Still doesn't. Hates the water now. Anyway, they were out in my old boat together. Ping's mother fell overboard. Fern didn't even know how to steer the damn thing or turn it around. Before she could do anything, Ping's mother drowned. She was a good swimmer"—Pingree took a suck from his cigarette—"so my guess is she hit her head when she went over, and knocked herself out."

At that point, the three of them were heading into Lunch. My mother. Jazzy. Georgette.

Here was Pingree talking to me man-to-man; here was my mother headed in to call me Johnny and say things like "Don't talk with your mouth full." ·

"So Ping and Fern don't get along too well," Pingree said. "My son is laughed at. I know that. It's my fault. He wants to be a magician because that's all he thinks he can change: one card into another, a handkerchief into a rose . . . Poor Ping. I want him to know he isn't trapped and that his life can be changed, too."

Jazzy'd even brought along the fancy clothes shoebox, easy to distinguish from the poor clothes one because there were red and silver sequins pasted on it.

"I have certain plans I'm going to keep from Fern."

"Like what?"

I kept my head down as though that would stop Mom from seeing me. That was ostrich thinking: Bury your head in the sand and no one's supposed to be able to see the rest of you.

"I'm going to find a way Ping won't have to go to Gardner, without Fern knowing anything about it."

"That'll be a neat trick."

My mother was inside then, telling her hostess there was her son, out on the terrace. I saw her pointing in my direction, saw the hostess step back to let Jazzy and my mother pass.

"That will indeed be a very neat trick," Pingree said. "And, Fell?"

"Yes?"

"Keep it under your hat. Can I trust you to do that?"

"Absolutely!"

Then my mother appeared on the porch, calling out, "Johnny? Look what the cat just dragged in!"

"Us!" Jazzy squealed. "We want screamers!"

"Oh, migosh," I said to Pingree. "This is embarrassing. My whole family's just shown up."

"Quite all right," he said. He looked toward my mother and Jazzy, heading our way. My mother liked to wear white in summer. She was in a white pants suit, with a white plastic bracelet. She had on white plastic earrings and white beads.

Jazzy had on her new Little Leaguer top, with red pants and red sneakers.

"Don't tell me *you're* Woodrow Pingree!" my mother exclaimed when she got to our table.

Pingree rose and stuck out his hand, the cigarette hanging on his lips.

"So we meet again," Pingree said.

"This is the mysterious Mr. X!" my mother said. She said to Pingree, "This is my son, Johnny . . . the one I told you all about . . . and all along you've known each other!"

"All along," Pingree said.

"You knew he was my son," said Mom.

"Yes, I knew."

Jazzy put Georgette down on the table, still dressed in her rags.

IT WAS NINE O'CLOCK.

I said, "I'm going to call my date and tell her I can't make it."

"I wish you'd keep your date, Fell," Pingree said.

"I don't know. I just don't know."

My mother was saying the same thing—"I don't know"—over and over. But it wasn't as if she were considering an idea that didn't appeal to her. There was that little light in her eyes, the sort that comes there at the prospect of a new store opening nearby, inviting the public to open charge accounts.

Pingree had suggested we all go back to our house. He'd waited until my mother put Jazzy to bed to drop the bomb. The saucer my mother'd given him for an ashtray was overflowing with butts. There was a smokey haze above the room. My mother got up to open another window and put on some lights. We'd been sitting in the living room listening while it got dark out.

I didn't know how I could go on a date and act normal

after someone had just offered to pay me twenty thousand dollars to become his son for two years.

"Let me get this straight," my mother said. "Johnny goes to this Gardner School as your son."

"Yes. My son's already been accepted there. I've already paid his tuition."

"Everyone at Gardner will know Johnny as your son."

"Exactly. Johnny will be Ping there." Pingree shook up a cigarette from the Viceroy package. He picked his lighter up from the table. "Gardner is in a very small town in Bucks County, Pennsylvania. The boys come from all over the United States, about seventy in all. Most of them rich kids. About fifty are old boys and twenty new ones." He lit the cigarette. "None from around here. I checked. None from Brooklyn. A lot of them are legacies, as Ping is. Their fathers and their grandfathers have all gone to Gardner."

My mother sat down on the leather hassock near the armchair where Pingree was sitting. He had his legs stretched out in front of him, relaxed, no hint in his voice or his posture that my mother's sudden arrival at Lunch had thrown him. He said it had. He said he hadn't counted on making this proposal quite yet. Then, with a shrug, he said so what if it was a little premature? We'd all need the extra time.

"Johnny will be Ping at Gardner," said my mother, "and Ping will go off to this school in Switzerland."

"L'Ecole la Coeur. Yes. Ping will be John Fell there."

"But what about my school transcripts?" I said.

"We'll have them forwarded to Switzerland. As I told

you, Ping will skip a year. Gladly. Ping hates school. And you'll repeat a year. You'll enter Gardner as a junior."

"I don't know," my mother said for about the fortieth time.

I said, "And I'm supposed to say I won a Brutt scholarship to go overseas to prep school?"

"That's the easiest part. Fern and I are on the search committee for those scholarships. We give several a year to worthy students. They study in France, Italy—all over the place. I usually do the interviewing and Fern okays my choices. Fern already likes you. She's for it. She thinks I was looking you over for the scholarship."

Mom said, "But she doesn't know Ping's going there in Johnny's place."

"No."

"But won't she write him, call him?"

"She's never called him. They aren't that close. She may write him once or twice. Johnny will forward the letters to Ping. Ping will send his to Johnny to mail. Ping rarely uses the telephone. But if he wants to call, Fern will think he's calling from Gardner."

I said, "But what if Keats wants to call me, Mr. Pingree?"

"Woody."

"Woody. What if Keats decides to call me? She *could*."

"Tell her L'Ecole la Coeur discourages transatlantic calls. That's all. You can call her, if you have to. She'll think you're in Switzerland. *But*"—Pingree dropped an ash into the saucer—"I'd cool this thing with the Keating girl. It's cooling anyway, isn't it? Her father led me to believe it was."

"She's the least of it!" said Mom.

"Mom, she's not the least of it."

"She is where I'm concerned. She's never treated you like anything but a toy."

"Well, that may change," Pingree said. "Girls treating you like a toy may change once you've had some Gardner polish. You'll come out of there a man."

"What am I now?"

"A boy," my mother said.

Pingree glanced down at his Rolex. "A boy with a date soon. I have to run along. You keep your date, Fell. We'll talk more about all this. . . . But how does it strike you, Mrs. Fell?"

Mom turned her palms up. "I wish I could understand why you can't just tell your wife you don't want your son to go to Gardner. He isn't even her son!"

"There are a lot of reasons I can't," said Pingree. "You have to know my wife, know a lot about her background, things I'm not privileged to reveal. People are complex, Mrs. Fell. And sometimes it comes down to little things, too, like the fact that my wife would hate to have Ping give up that twenty thousand left for him in the will. My wife is very parsimonious."

"Par-si-what?"

"Parsimonious, Mom. The opposite of what you are. Careful with a buck."

Mom shot me a look. Pingree smiled. He said, "Yes. Fern is careful with a buck. She's also convinced that

I've spoiled Ping. She talked me into sending him off to this military school he hated."

"If you ask me," Mom said, "you've let her push you around."

"Agreed," said Pingree. "The heart has its reasons."

"Isn't she going to find out anyway, someday? She'll wonder where the twenty thousand went, won't she? And you have to pay Ping's tuition in Switzerland?"

"Only half. The scholarship takes care of the rest. I have the money set aside to cover all that, Mrs. Fell . . . and if she finds out someday, well"—Pingree shrugged—"I'll handle it then."

"What about vacations?" I asked.

"What about them? You'll come home at Christmas, spring break, and summers, as Ping will."

"They'll probably speak French at that school in Switzerland," I said. "People will expect me to rattle off French."

"They speak English and French at L'Ecole la Coeur. But after Gardner," said Pingree, "you'll be able to rattle off French. You'll get a first-rate education, far better than Ping will get at that country club he's going to. But Ping can't wait to get away."

"And he knows I'll get the twenty thousand?"

"He knows you'll get ten thousand at the end of your junior year, and ten when you graduate, yes. Ping doesn't give a hoot about money. But the Gardner diploma will be in his name—*I* care about that, strangely enough. Our family has always come out of Gardner."

"And I'll have this diploma from a country club."

"A diploma that will surely impress all your customers in your fancy restaurant one day." Pingree smiled at me. Then he stood up. "It's time for your date, isn't it?"

"I have to call her," I said.

Mom said, "You've given us a lot to think about."

"We'll work things out," said Pingree. "When you decide, if it's a go-ahead, we'll start by getting Fell's passport."

"Is Ping going to use my passport? We don't look at all alike."

"No. Ping will travel with his own passport. You won't use yours. We'll work out all the details, don't worry."

Mom said, "What an opportunity it would be for you, Johnny!"

I just couldn't believe the offer was for real.

"Remember what I told you when I first came into Dressed to Kill?" Pingree said to Mom. "Your fate is set. Just lean into it."

"I hope those pants fit," Mom said.

"They're too young for me, Mrs. Fell. I didn't go in your store for pants."

Mom walked him toward the door. "I thought you were this lonely man, just interested in hearing about my family."

"I *was* interested in all you had to say about Fell."

11

IT WAS CLOSE TO TEN O'CLOCK when I got down to the place where Delia Tremble was an au pair.

On the phone she'd told me it wouldn't be much of a date. The family she worked for went out, so she couldn't leave. She said she was tired, too, and hungry, and there wasn't anything in the house but eggs.

I said I didn't feel like much of a date, anyway. I was tired, too, and I could do fantastic things with eggs.

It was a big stone house near the ocean, the kind with the front facing the dunes. When I walked in the door, the kitchen was right there on the left. Delia Tremble steered me that way.

"I ate about five, with the kids," she said. "Then the Stileses had lobster, which I hate, and now I feel like something sweet and there's only eggs."

"Is there bread?"

"Yes, a whole loaf."

"How about French toast?"

"Can you make it? I love it!"

I watched while she cleared away a cup of coffee and an ashtray from the butcher block table. She was wearing skintight jeans and spiked heels, with a white cotton sweater. Her earrings were tiny gold hoops and she wore several gold rings.

She looked back at me and smiled. "Do you really know how to make French toast, because I can hardly cook?"

"I like that." I smiled and began rolling up the sleeves of my plaid shirt.

"What? That I can hardly cook?"

"Yeah, because I really like to."

"Be my guest." She laughed, pointing to the stove.

She got a carton of eggs out of the refrigerator and slid a loaf of bread down the counter. She was tall; with her high heels, as tall as I was. Her hair was very black and very long, touching her shoulders.

"I'll need a bowl and a frying pan. I hope you have milk and butter."

"I'm glad you came, Fell. I wasn't looking forward to it, but now I'm glad you came."

"The way to a woman's heart is through her stomach."

"Usually not." She laughed again, and I looked at her waistline and figured she was telling the truth. She didn't look like someone who lived to eat. She looked like someone who lived to dance or play tennis or swim. She had a good tan. She almost had dimples when she smiled. Very long black eyelashes, a straight nose, and straight white teeth.

I beat the eggs and milk, and added a little salt and sugar.

"I can't believe you're doing this," she said. "It seems strange to have someone you don't even know walk in and just start making you French toast."

"Everything that's happening to me lately seems strange," I said.

"Do you want to talk about it?" I heard her scratch a match, and smelled a fresh cigarette.

"No, I don't want to talk about it."

"Is this how we're going to begin? With you keeping secrets from me?"

"Yes," I said. "Tell me about Delia Tremble." I put the slices of bread into the liquid.

"I look younger than I am. I never tell my age. I like serious guys who are good talkers."

"What do you like to talk about?" I put some heat on under the frying pan and dropped in some oil and some butter.

"I like the way people talk on planes," she said. "They just start in telling you about themselves."

"Do you know why that is? It's because people on planes don't have the scenery people on buses and trains have to distract them."

"Is that true?"

"My father used to be a detective. He said you could travel more unnoticed on a train. People don't look at you as closely."

"I never thought of that, Fell."

"Okay," I said, "we're on a plane. Start talking." I

raised the heat and waited for the frying pan to get hot.

"When I first noticed you in Plain and Fancy I figured you for one of these prep school kids. A preppy. I figured you came from money."

"Were you wrong!"

"Do you go to high school?"

"Umm hmm." I dropped the bread into the pan. "I'll need some paper towels in a minute. Were you after my money?"

"Maybe." I liked her laugh. "I liked the way you moved, too. I figured you'd be a good dancer."

"And that we could dance outdoors. That's what you said you wanted. To dance outdoors. Why outdoors?"

"Because I smoke," she said. "People are really getting to hate us smokers."

"So that's why," I said, and she came up behind me and reached around me to put down some paper towels.

"Did you ever smoke? Do you drink?" she asked.

"I used to do both," I said. "Name it, I did it."

"I'm glad you don't drink now. I don't really like men who do."

I noticed the "men." Keats still said "boys."

I said, "Do you go to boarding school or high school?"

"I graduated from high school."

"Oh," I said, "an older woman."

"Not that much older than you are. I was ahead of everyone."

"Are you going to college?"

"I want to travel. I haven't been many places. Have you been many places, Fell?"

"Not many at all."

"Oh, Fell, it looks good!"

I dropped the fried bread on the paper towels. "Jam, or maple syrup?"

"Maple syrup," she said. "I'll get it from the cupboard. Will you go to high school again next year?"

"Maybe," I said. "Or maybe I'll go away to school. I might get a scholarship. I might go to Switzerland."

"I want to hear all about it!"

"I'm not going to talk about it. It's bad luck to talk about something that hasn't come through yet."

She had out plates and I put the French toast on them.

She said, "Let's take this into the living room. If the twins wake up, I can hear them better from in there."

I followed her, carrying some forks and napkins she handed me.

"Are you a happy type, Fell?"

"What do you mean?"

"Just what I said. Are you a sad type or a happy type?"

I watched her bend over to put the plates down on the marble coffee table in front of this long, beige sofa. I saw the movement of her breasts under her white sweater.

"Right now I'm a happy type." I said.

"When were you last sad?"

"The last time? When my father died."

"That makes sense."

"And you?"

We sat down side by side on the sofa.

"Sometimes I get a melancholy feeling out here, so

close to the ocean, not really connected with anyone in Seaville. I think the beach brings out a sadness in you, if you're alone. But it never stays with me. It comes and goes."

"Now you know me, so you're not alone anymore."

"Now I do." She took a taste of the French toast. "You're a good cook, aren't you, Fell?"

"Yes."

"And what else about you?"

I put up one hand. "Don't rush us."

She looked over at me. She wasn't smiling. "Oh, Fell, I like that you said that. That's the best thing you've said all night. Do you mean it?"

"I do." I did. I wanted to take my time with her. I liked the way she looked, and I liked her style. She was easier than Keats, wiser, less manic-depressive. I liked what she'd said about being at the beach alone, and the sadness it brought out in you. Keats wouldn't have had the good sense to figure that out. She always made any sadness into something she was doing wrong, into failing and spending her life on nothing.

"We should have some music on, I guess," Delia Tremble said.

"We don't need it."

"What do you like?"

"Everything, but I don't know anything about classical stuff."

"I don't either. I like Whitney Houston. I like songs I can hear the lyrics in more than I like hard rock, and I don't like heavy metal."

She was telling me the names of singers and songs she liked when I happened to look across the room and see this painting of the ocean. Down in the lower right was the familiar fern.

I waited until she was finished talking. Then I said, "This family you work for . . ."

"The Stileses."

"Did they buy that painting?"

"Mrs. Stiles owns the Stiles Gallery in town. One of her artists did that."

"Fern Pingree," I said.

"Do you know her?"

"Not well."

"How come you know her, Fell?"

I told her that I had dated a girl who lived next door to the Pingrees.

"What does she say about this Fern Pingree?"

"She doesn't know her."

"I'd be curious about her."

"Would be or are?"

"You listen too carefully sometimes, Fell. I would be, if I lived around here. She'd be someone I'd be curious about if I lived in Seaville."

"Why?"

"Look at that painting."

I looked again. It was an angry-looking ocean, with another sun above it that looked hot enough to fry eggs on the sand. There was a haze over the whole scene, the kind of whiteness that comes over a beach on a sizzling day when the sun just breaks through the clouds.

"Do you know what she named that painting?" Delia Tremble asked. "*Arizona Darkness*. Figure that one out!"

We both laughed.

Delia leaned back against the couch cushions. We were silent for a while. You could hear the sounds of the sea off in the distance. Delia was twirling a strand of her black hair around her finger.

"Fell? If you could have one wish now, what would it be?"

"That I could see you tomorrow."

She smiled at me. "Not tomorrow. They're having company. But maybe Monday night."

"And what would you wish for?"

"What would I wish for?" She thought about it for a while. "I want to get away. I want to travel."

Then we heard the Stileses arriving, heard Mrs. Stiles say, "Something smells good!"

"I told you it wouldn't be much of a date, Fell," Delia Tremble said.

I said quickly, "If you'd like to travel, how about traveling out to the Surf Club with me Monday night? You can dance outdoors there."

She said okay.

12

I'M ALL FOR THE IDEA [Mom had written]. *You'll get a good education, money to use for college or a restaurant, and don't you think your father would want you to go? I've thought and thought and I vote yes! Jazzy and I are at church. Meat loaf for dinner is cooling, don't put in fridge. . . . I think you should tell Mr. Pingree you'll do it, before he changes his mind!*

But I wanted to think about it, and talk more about it, and figure out how the whole scheme would work.

"All right," Pingree said, "but don't take too long to decide. If I can't get you to take the offer, I'll have to think of someone else."

Pingree watched me through a cloud of his own cigarette smoke.

We were sitting out on the front porch of the Frog Pond, having Sunday breakfast. He'd called early and I had said I'd meet him at ten. I couldn't sleep late, anyway. I usually liked to, when Mom took Jazzy to church and I didn't have to get up, but I couldn't. I woke up thinking about going to Gardner as Ping, and

I laughed aloud at the idea. I thought of the way kids back in Brooklyn would say "Farrrr out!"

I kept thinking about Delia Tremble when I first woke up, too. I kept remembering the look in her dark eyes when she talked about sadness. I even got out of bed, pulled on my shorts, and tried to reach Keats at Four Winds. I guess I was guilty because I'd awakened thinking of someone else. Finally. After a year!

But Keats wasn't around. They rang that cow bell of theirs and shouted, "Keats! Keats! Keats!" She wasn't around. The girl who answered the phone asked me if I was Quint. I said yeah, Quint. She said someone just told her Keats was on her way to my motel; she'd left about ten minutes ago.

"You seem distracted this morning, Fell," Pingree said. "Or are you just a sad type?"

I remembered Delia asking me if I was a happy type or a sad type.

"You ought to know the answer to that. You've done enough research on me."

"All right. You're not yourself this morning. Why?"

"I can't imagine going through two years answering to the name Ping."

"You don't have to answer to that name. You can be Woodrow. Woody. My middle name is Thompson. You can be Thompson, Tom."

"Just kidding," I said.

"I don't like Ping, either. No one ever called *me* that."

There was a young couple behind Pingree who looked as if they'd just left a bedroom somewhere and it was too soon, because they couldn't stop touching each other. I remembered what that was like back last year when Keats and I would go anyplace. We couldn't keep our hands off each other. What was the word Pingree'd used to describe falling in love? He'd said he was besotted. I'd looked it up later in my Webster's. It meant mentally stupefied, silly, foolish.

Pingree looked around to see what I was looking at. He shook his head as though he knew what that was like, too.

He gave me a wistful smile. "Do you miss Keats?"

"I miss her. But I don't think she misses me. I might take your advice. I might cool it with Keats." I'd already decided not to go up to Four Winds for the play. Let Quint Blade go.

"Good!" he said. "Cool it."

"Not because I'm taking you up on your offer."

"All right. It's probably still a good idea."

"I can't trust her."

"Can she trust you?"

"I don't know, after last night."

"I forgot about last night. How did it go?"

"Fine."

"You liked her?"

"She was easy to talk to. She likes to talk."

I watched the couple kiss. Everyone out on the porch was watching them. The waitress was standing there with orange juice on a tray, grinning, waiting for room to put the juice down in front of them. I counted to five, slowly. They were still at it.

Pingree said, "Let me tell you about this club at Gardner."

"Another thing," I interrupted him. "What if I get a thing for Delia Tremble?"

"If it's 'a thing,' it won't matter, will it?"

"You know what I mean. What if I fall for Delia Tremble?"

"Write her. That's what you'd do anyway, isn't it? She's not from Seaville, is she?"

"No."

"Well then?"

"But I'd want to see her."

Pingree stabbed some bacon with his fork. "You can't have everything you want. You can have a lot, but not everything. No one can ever have everything!"

I looked out at this fat pigeon waddling around on the green lawn, and bit into my English muffin. I said, "What club were you going to tell me about?"

"It's called Sevens. It's a secret club at Gardner. It's *the* club."

"Like a fraternity?"

"No. No. It's not like anything you've ever heard about. They have their own rules, their own privileges. They control The Tower there."

"Why do they call it Sevens?"

"No one knows."

"What do you mean, no one knows? Someone must know."

"Members of Sevens know what it means, of course.

My grandfather knew. He was the only member from our family."

"Did he tell you anything about it?"

"Never! If you get into Sevens you never tell the reason you got in, or the meaning of the name, or anything about Sevens. You're set apart when you get into Sevens . . . some say for life."

"You didn't make it, and your father didn't?"

"Just my grandfather."

"Why are you mentioning it this morning?"

"There's something else I didn't tell you about my grandfather's will," he said. He finished his bacon and eggs, pushed his plate back, and lit a cigarette. "If you make Sevens, you automatically get another ten thousand dollars. You get it instantly."

"You didn't think I'd make it, so you didn't mention it before, hmmm?" I couldn't eat any more. I tossed the rest of the muffin out toward the fat pigeon on the lawn.

Pingree began to speak extra clearly, as though he wanted what he was saying to really sink in.

"No one knows why a boy qualifies for Sevens. There's no type. Anyone can be in Sevens, but few are. Only about five or six a year. One year there was no one tapped for Sevens."

"This club really impresses you, doesn't it? You're not just talking about it because of the extra ten thousand, are you?"

"Yes, I guess it does really impress me, Fell. I like

solutions to things. I could never solve that one—what makes a Sevens."

"If I were to go to Gardner, and if I got in, I'd tell you."

"Oh, no. No one's ever been told."

"But I think that stuff is crap! I don't care about secret clubs!"

"Gardner will teach you about tradition. Tradition isn't a bad thing, Fell. Sometimes it's the only continuity."

"I don't mean tradition. I like tradition, too." I did. So had my dad. Christmas used to be this big production when he was alive, starting with the tree trimming on Christmas Eve. He always made Christmas breakfast, too. "It's snobbery I don't like. It's people thinking they're better than other people just because they're in some stupid club."

"I see."

He stirred his coffee. We both checked out the lovers. They were still at it. Pingree met my eyes and we grinned.

Then Pingree said, "I wish I'd been more like you when I was growing up. I was all caught up in what it meant to be a Pingree, what was expected of me. My father drilled that into me. I've done a lot of bad things to Ping, but I'll never do that to him. I'm surprised Fern isn't more sympathetic in this regard. She hates snobbery, too, but she's dead set on Ping's going to Gardner. Ping can't conquer that phobia of his. We've tried hypnotism, everything. I think Fern thinks he's faking it."

I said, "I saw *Arizona Darkness* last night."

He looked across at me. "That belongs to the Stileses."

"Delia Tremble's their au pair."

"Ah! For the twins."

"Yes. We wondered why your wife named something *Arizona Darkness* that's this ocean under this hot sun?"

"She chooses very unusual titles for her paintings. I think that one had to do with Jerome, Arizona. Oh, they all do, really."

"What does Jerome, Arizona, have to do with your wife?"

Pingree ground out his cigarette in the ashtray. "Her grandfather was there in World War Two, long before she was born. They had one of those internment camps there for Japanese-Americans. Our version of concentration camps. We didn't gas them the way the Germans did the Jews. Didn't work them. But we confined them. They were our prisoners. Only Japanese-Americans were put through that. Fern can't forget it."

I remembered watching a program about it on TV.

"I didn't even know she was Japanese."

"Her father is. Not her mother. Her mother's Irish-American."

I was remembering the barracks in the field, in the painting she called *Smiles We Left Behind Us.*

"Then came Hiroshima, another shattering blow to Asians. And Vietnam. Fern has a very melancholy nature as a result. I fall in love with very melancholy women. My first wife was the same way."

I liked him. I wasn't sure why. Maybe because he never talked down to me.

He called for the check.

"There's so little time," he said. "You know that, don't you, Fell?"

13

ON THE WAY to the Surf Club Monday night, Delia Tremble said she wanted a frozen custard. I stopped at Frosty's, and she passed two dollars to me and said, "Get yourself one, too, Hunk!"

I took the money.

I said, "This doesn't mean you can have your way with me later."

She had that lilting laugh I'd grown to love in just forty-eight hours. The sky was deep blue with an orange ball up in it, and a thousand stars. We were headed down to the club to dance outside under them. She smelled of roses, or she reminded me of how roses smell. I didn't know which.

When I came back with two chocolate frozen custards dripping down my fingers, she said, "Why do you carry a gun?"

"Why do you snoop into my glove compartment?"

"You go first," she said.

"It's my dad's gun."

It was his .38 Smith & Wesson, never loaded, with ivory butt plates and an owl carved into it, the eyes made of two real rubies. Years ago some Mafia character'd given it to him as thanks for following his wife around.

She said, "But he's dead, you said."

I got behind the wheel. "I can't throw it out or turn it in."

"So you keep it in your car?"

"My dad did, too. He said you should never keep a gun in the house. A lot of accidents with guns happen in policemen's houses, did you know that?"

"No." She was licking the frozen custard off the side of the cone. It was sexy the way she did that.

"A lot of homicides happen in policemen's homes, too," I said. "Their guns are always there." I put a napkin around the bottom of my cone. It wasn't going to do any good. It was a hot night. I was glad to be with her.

"Now your turn," I said. "What were you looking for in my glove compartment?"

"Any evidence I could find of you."

"Why?"

"I'm curious about you."

"Are you glad I'm not the preppy you thought I was?"

"I like preppies."

"What do you like about them?"

"I like the ones who go to all-male schools."

"Why them?"

"They're starved for women, so they're eager to please

and shyer, but they have more dignity than other guys."
She bit into the tip of the chocolate custard. "I like all
three traits."

"You like eager to please, shy, and dignified?"

"Yes. Are you any of those?"

"I'm eager to please, and I'm dignified."

"I'll make you shy," she said.

I laughed painfully. "It's worth a try." I managed to
sound my idea of suave. Maybe not hers. I started the
car.

"Could you ever use that gun?"

"I could. I know how to shoot. I learned to shoot
when I was thirteen."

"Guns scare me," she said, "but they fascinate me,
too. This is awful. When I saw that gun in there, it
turned me on."

"*This* is awful," I said. "It turns me on that it turned
you on."

We both laughed. I took her left hand with my right.

I wished I had a convertible. We should have been
speeding down toward the sea in a convertible. I'd never
had that kind of thought with Keats. I suppose that was
because there was only one thing I could do with Keats
that Daddy and she hadn't already done, including speed
along Ocean Road in a little blue Benz, top down. But
with Delia Tremble I felt there were things I could show
her, maybe not then and there, but there was the feeling
she hadn't seen it all. She'd already said she hadn't been
many places. Keats had been to Europe three times,

India, the Orient, even China. I couldn't begin to name all the islands in the Caribbean she'd carried her tube of Bain de Soleil down to and come back bronze from.

Delia let go of my hand and reached into her pocket for a cigarette. I pushed in the lighter. She had on a bright-blue cotton blazer with the sleeves rolled up, over a dress with big blue and white flowers all over it. The same hoop earrings; the same gold rings. She had white low-heeled sandals on, so she was shorter than I was this time.

I had on some khaki stone-washed pants that Keats had given me last summer. It seemed like way back last summer with Delia beside me and something new starting. Something good.

When the lighter popped out, I held it up for her.

"Thanks," she said. "Fell? Do you miss anyone now?"

"No. Do you?"

"Not now. Thanks for taking me dancing, Fell."

I couldn't remember any girl ever thanking me for taking her somewhere, on the way there.

She shifted her cigarette to her right hand and held my right hand again.

I looked over at her. I decided to try out my father's old imitation of Humphrey Bogart. I sucked down my lower lip and said, "This is just the beginning of our travels, kid."

"Don't," she said.

"Don't what?"

"Do the Bogie bit. I don't like bits. I always think men pull that stuff when they're afraid to show any emotion."

So *there*, Dad.

I said, "Why shouldn't we be afraid to show emotion? Show emotion and die."

"No. That's see Naples. See Naples and die." She laughed. "Show emotion and take your chances."

Delia Tremble was a real good dancer. When you danced with her, people watched. Not you. Her. Some people watched her and danced. A few couples stopped to watch her.

She had all sorts of moves, and she'd heard every song whether it was a hard rock disco song or the softer kind that came rarely and only at the end of a set. She did things with herself that were graceful and hot and new to me. New to a lot of us. What I liked was she didn't dance for them, and she didn't dance for herself like some girls do. Some girls dance in a way you could go down to the corner and back and they wouldn't know you'd been gone. Delia danced for me, and with me, smiling at me, her eyes always coming back to me.

We danced out on the big deck, without sitting down, for about an hour.

Then we went into the bar, got some cherry Cokes, and took them outside to the little deck and talked for another hour.

She told me she was from Atlantic City. Her father

had once managed a big hotel there when Atlantic City was still pretty much a summer resort.

"When I was a kid," she said, "I used to wait for winter, when all the tourists would be gone. Then my mom and my sisters and I could move into one of the big suites that looked out on the ocean. That's why the ocean here affects me so. It reminds me of when I was little."

A red-faced, crew-cut older guy began playing piano on the little deck.

Delia said, "Let's dance here. On the lawn. It's slow. We can take off our shoes. It's wet on the grass."

We did.

I knew the song the fellow began singing. It was an old, old Billy Joel one, from before he'd met Christie Brinkley. It was one he wrote to his first wife about not changing, and it used to get Mom mad. It said he didn't need clever conversation, he wanted her to stay the way she was. Mom would say, "Stay dumb, huh? Is that the message, Billy Joel?"

But it sounded really romantic with this old saloon singer doing it. He sounded as if he were an inch away from having lung cancer. He was smoking, no hands, the way Pingree often did. He was singing "Don't go changing."

We were dancing out there on the wet grass by ourselves, in the dark. I kissed her near the end of the song. She kissed me back.

I think we both felt changed, never mind don't go

changing, because we didn't smile or joke as we walked back toward the deck. You could cut the tension with a knife. It was sex. It was this great physical thirst that had come over us, and that we knew was coming, but weren't sure what to do with after its arrival.

We sat down on the steps and picked up our cherry Cokes.

Delia said, "I have a chance to go around the world in the fall. On a ship. I'm going to take it."

"Will you be an au pair?"

"Not for the Stileses."

"Did you just decide?"

"Not *just*. About a month ago. I wasn't sure I wanted to go away for such a long time."

"How long?"

"A year at least."

I let out a low whistle instead of a wail.

"I wanted to tell you," she said. "I was going to wait to tell you, but now I think you should know."

"A year?"

"Yes."

She put her hand over mine. "I feel things, too, Fell. The way you dance."

"The way *I* dance," I said.

She took her hand away and reached for a cigarette.

"Thanks for not being mean about my smoking, too."

I smelled her light up. She smoked those long brown Mores.

I finally said, "I might go away myself."

"Really? Where?"

"I told you. Switzerland. Prep school."

"Oh, Fell, you'd be a preppy after all."

"Don't laugh."

"I'm not. I told you. I like that."

"I like you," I said, "and I think I know what you're saying."

"What am I saying?"

"You're saying we both feel something. *But.*" I took her hand and brought it up to my lips, and let my tongue play lightly between her fingers. Then I put her hand back. "You're saying we can't help feeling it, but we can't expect to make anything out of it. Nothing permanent for now."

"Nothing permanent. Exactly. Because I'll be away a long time."

"I will be, too," I said.

I decided then and there to go to Gardner.

We danced an hour longer. I never danced that way before with anyone, never felt that way with anyone while I was dancing.

Then we drove down to the beach. We were still there when the sun started coming up.

Tuesday was her day off.

I said, "Come home with me. I'll make us breakfast. You can meet my mother and Jazzy."

She ran her finger down my lips, then pressed them together with it. "Hush, Fell."

She had the collar of the blue blazer turned up and my aqua sweater wrapped around her neck like a scarf.

For once, I wasn't at all cold.

"I don't want to meet your family, or get to know your friends. I don't want ties. I don't want us to be a couple."

"What are we then?" I wasn't whining around as I used to with Keats. I was asking her to see what she'd come up with, after what had just happened between us.

"We're what we are, Fell." She smiled. She looked sleepy. "We don't have to define it or label it . . . and I want our memories to be just of the two of us."

I kept trying to keep myself from making some kind of wisecrack, or doing a Bogie imitation, or all the other jazz. She'd taught me that.

She took my hand. "I like what we are," she said. "It's good enough, isn't it?"

"It's better than that," I said.

We left the beach, and I dropped her off at the Stileses'.

When I got home, I called Woodrow Pingree and told him I'd decided to do it.

"You won't be sorry, Fell," he said.

PART TWO

ARIZONA DARKNESS

14

THE FIRST THING I found out was that no one going to Gardner School ever called it that. They called it The Hill. The school sat on a hill in the middle of farm country. That was all I saw, once I got off the train at Trenton, New Jersey, and into the school bus. Ten of us new boys were bound for the little town of Cottersville, Pennsylvania.

There we were met by a dozen fellows in light-blue blazers and navy-blue pants. All the blazers had gold 7's over the blue-and-white Gardner insignias. The group formed a seven around us and sang the Gardner song.

> Others will fill our places,
> Dressed in the old light blue.
> We'll recollect our races.
> We'll to the flag be true.
> And youth will still be in our faces
> When we cheer for a Gardner crew . . .

And youth will still be in our faces
When we cheer for a Gardner crew!

A fellow behind me said, "Now we have to plant trees."

"We have to what?"

"We each have to plant a tree. It's the first thing you do when you get here, even before you get your room assigned. You get a little evergreen handed to you. You have to give it a name."

"What kind of a name?"

"Any name. A name. By the way, I'm Sidney Dibble. Dib."

"I'm Thompson Pingree. Tom."

He was the basketball player type, all legs and arms, skinny, so tall I had to look way up at him. He was blond like me. He had on a tan suit with a beige T-shirt and Reeboks.

I'd worn the only suit that had been mine in my other life: the dark-blue one. I felt like Georgette after her real family had come to claim her. Pingree had driven me into New York City one August afternoon and taken me to Brooks Brothers. I had a whole trunkful of new stuff.

I asked Dib if he was sure about this tree thing. That was one detail Pingree'd left out. Dib said he was positive. His brother'd just graduated from Gardner. Dib said he was the world's foremost authority on Gardner—"Except when it comes to Sevens," he added.

The words weren't even out of his mouth a half second before a member of Sevens began barking orders at us. He was a tall skinhead, with vintage thrift-shop zoot-suit pants, and two earrings in his left ear. He had on a pair of black Converse sneakers.

"My name is Creery! Leave your luggage on the ground! It will be in your room when you get there! We will now walk back to Gardner Woods for the tree-planting ceremony! Think of a name for your tree on the way. Whatever you wish to call it. After you have planted your tree, you will line up to receive your room assignments in The Tower!"

"Who's the punk rocker?" I asked Dib. "I thought Sevens was this exclusive club?"

"He just told you. His name is Cyril Creery."

"And *he's* a Sevens?"

"There's no predicting who'll make Sevens. But he's easy. It's a guy named Lasher you don't want on your case . . . unless *you* make Sevens. Then he can't touch you. Creery and Lasher hate each other. When Creery first got here, Lasher hated the sight of him. Creery had hair then. Purple hair. Lasher was out to get him. You know, Creery's the kind that named his tree Up Yours! Lasher would have made his life hell here, but Creery made Sevens."

"Don't the other members have a say in who makes Sevens?"

"I don't know how it works. No one does."

"Maybe you need three blackballs, like in a fraternity."

"Nobody knows," Dib said.

Besides the ten of us who'd gotten off the train in Trenton, there were ten other new boys already at The Hill. Now there were twenty of us walking to Gardner Woods.

There we found twenty holes in two rows, with twenty shovels beside them, and twenty mounds of dirt.

There was a line forming to receive the evergreens.

"You tell Creery the name of your tree, then stick it in the ground and throw the dirt over it," Dib said. "I'm going to name mine after my dog, Thor."

"Are all those trees in the background from classes ahead of us?"

"You've got it. What are you naming yours?"

"I'm not sure yet."

"You better have a name ready when we get up there."

I thought of naming mine Delia. But that wouldn't have been the way we'd agreed to be. Nothing permanent. A tree was pretty permanent. I thought of all the names people called their houses down on Dune Road in Seaville. I thought of Adieu. I thought of Keats's saying on Labor Day, "Daddy says you can come here as long as you've come to say good-bye." I told her she could tell Daddy to shove it! Keats said, "Oh, my, my, my. Aren't we arrogant now that we're going abroad to school. Do you kiss arrogantly now, too?" I didn't kiss her good-bye arrogantly, but I did try to get something simulating emotion into it. Nothing. Delia'd have laughed. She'd have said, "What did you think, Fell, that you could forget me?" She was already gone by the time

Keats came back from Four Winds. But Delia was never going to be gone.

I said to Dib, "I may name mine Adieu."

"Oh, oui?" He laughed.

I thought of how I'd razzed Keats because Adieu had sounded pretentious. Why not just good-bye? I'd said. Why the French?

"No, not Adieu," I said. "Good-bye."

"Your tree's going to be called Good-bye?"

"It's as good as Thor, isn't it?"

"Sure. Call it anything. You know this guy Lasher I told you about? My brother says he puts on this big act. He wants to be a playwright. He writes these plays with characters in them named Death and Destruction, like he thinks he's profound, but it's all a lot of bullticky crap! I mean, he's a vegetarian, and he works out, and he's this big hypochondriac, but he's always playing with nooses and pretending he's being called to the grave. Well, he named his tree Suicide."

"I'm going to call mine Good-bye."

Good-bye to John Fell and his life, but not good-bye to Delia Tremble. We were going to write. "Promise," she'd said, "and if you don't like to write letters, or if you think you probably won't write me once you get there, tell me right now. I don't want false expectations."

I said I'd write. I promised.

Keats'd said, "Are we going to write ever?"

"I don't know," I'd said.

"Do you know you've changed since June? I'm going to think you've met someone else."

I couldn't tell her about it.

I was afraid I'd jinx it if I told anyone about Delia. "Jinx *what*?" my mother'd said. "She's going away for a year and all July and August you never knew when you were going to see her."

"Men! Plant your trees!" Creery shouted after we'd all been given an evergreen.

Men? The last time I'd ever been in on a tree planting was back in grade school in Brooklyn one Arbor Day. We'd all sung "This Land Is Your Land!" and walked around this little cherry tree holding hands.

Something about being one of ten boys in line with silver shovels and our holes already dug for us, with ten of the same behind us, reminded me of third grade.

But later, what happened in The Tower, didn't.

He said Sevens were always called by their last names, so I would call him Lasher. Everyone else on The Hill, except for faculty, was called by their first name. Good, I thought! No Pingree.

He said I'd been assigned to him. I was in his group. If I ever needed anything, I'd ask him if I could have it.

He had very thick glasses, like Ping's. He had thick, coal-black hair like Delia's, but his was cut very short. He had one of those almost beards—stubble, really—and a stubble mustache. A smile that tipped to one side.

How much older than me? A year maybe. Maybe my age. Seventeen. But I was sixteen at Gardner School. I

wasn't a Gemini anymore, either. I was a horny Scorpio.
Don't ask me how Ping could be a Scorpio with all the
sex appeal of a can opener, but he was. So was I, now.

Lasher said, "What'd you name your tree?"

"Good-bye."

"Good-bye's its name or are you a smartass?"

"That's its name."

We were way up in The Tower. We had to go up one
at a time, alphabetically. One hundred and twenty steps.
The stairs were stone ones on the outside. Even if you
didn't have a fear of heights it wasn't a climb that set
your heart to singing.

In the top of The Tower was this one stone-walled
room, lit by a single candle on the table. Lasher sat at
the table. There was nowhere for me to sit. I stood.
Lasher had on a white tank top under his blazer.

"Thompson, I want to tell you something. Don't screw
up! You've been assigned to me. I hate having scumbags
who come here and can't take it or can't make it! I happen to hate legacies, too—types like Creery, whose father
and grandfather went here, and miraculously all got to
be Sevens! I happen to love this place . . . *and* Sevens!
It's a privilege to be here, not a right! Act like you wanted
to come here more than you wanted to get laid the first
time, and we'll get along."

"I'll do that."

"You have gotten yourself laid by now, haven't you?"

"Yes, I have."

"Good. I won't have to cart you out to Willing Wanda's to get laid. I don't like virgins under my charge.

Virgins are vulnerable. I don't like vulnerable scumbags under my charge! *Latet anguis in herba*, Thompson! Do you know your Latin?"

"I don't know what that means."

"It's from Virgil. It means the snake hides in the grass. It's my motto."

"Okay," I said.

I could see that the gold buttons on his blazer had little 7's on them.

Then he said, "Seven Seas: the Arctic and the Antarctic. North and South Pacific. North and South Atlantic. The Indian Ocean."

I didn't know what that meant. I stood there.

"If a Sevens meets you he might ask you to name seven things that go together. If you can't think of seven things that go together, he might ask you to clean all the toilets in Hull House, where you'll be living. He might ask you to do anything, if you can't come up with seven things, and you'll have to do it!"

"All right," I said. "I'll find seven things for an answer."

"Find a lot of seven things. You can't repeat."

"All right."

"Your roommate is sixteen. He's from New Hope, Pennsylvania. He's a legacy, too."

"Okay," I said.

Lasher took off his thick glasses while he continued and talked with his eyes shut, as though he was bored out of his gourd but he had to get through this.

"Your roommate is a virgin. Your roommate called

me sir all through his interview. Your roommate named his tree after his puppy dog. He lets people call him Dib, a boy's nickname. He's obviously still on Pablum, so grow him up, Thompson, because your roommate's a vulnerable scumbag who doesn't realize *latet anguis*— finish it, Thompson!" He opened his eyes and looked up at me.

"In the grass . . . *in herba*."

So I was rooming with Sidney Dibble.

Lasher gave me this smile that was as beautiful as he was, without those thick glasses.

"Welcome to The Hill!" Lasher said.

John Fell
L'Ecole la Coeur
C H—1092 Rolle
Lake Geneva
Switzerland

Dear F
     E
       L

        L [I liked the way she wrote my name falling down], *I'll never forget our last dinner at The Frog Pond, remember? You were so sunburned you couldn't lean back in your chair. I liked it because you had to lean toward me.*

I know we said we wouldn't write about ordinary happenings—my idea, because I want our memories to be of what we shared together, but I want to know certain things about you . . . if you like where you are . . . if you are glad you made the choice to go to Switzerland. . . . You must tell me those things. . . . Tell me a thought you haven't told anyone. I won't tell you about life on this ship, except

*to say one port is like the next, and I think of you. I
remember once you combed your hair after we were down on
the beach. You put the comb in your back pocket, looked
over at me and said, "Do I look all right?" I love it that you
gave me that unguarded moment. "Do I look all right?"
you asked me. . . . I don't write long letters, F*

                                    E

                                        L

                                          L,

but I think long thoughts. Love, Delia.

The envelope Ping had sent it in was addressed to
W. Thompson Pingree, Gardner School, Cottersville,
Pennsylvania, U.S.A.

There were two letters from my mother inside. Even
she had to write to me in Switzerland, where Ping would
forward her mail. Pingree had insisted.

There was also a note from Ping.

> *Your French is improving,*
> *but you are avoiding all courses in computer science.*
> *How am I doing?*
> *Have I been up in The Tower yet?*

I was rereading my mail in Hull House on a Sunday
morning in October, anxious to get a letter off to Delia
before "my father" arrived. It was Pingree's first visit.
He was going to chapel with me.

"Just think," Dib said behind me, "right now, in that
luxurious clubhouse in the bottom of The Tower, there's
the aroma of rib roast cooking for the Sevens to enjoy

after chapel! They'll have rib roast, mashed potatoes. We'll be lucky to have chicken again. They've got it made, haven't they?"

"One thing I'm sick of," I said, "is everyone's obsession with the Sevens! God, who are they that everyone runs around in awe of them?"

"Wouldn't you like to be one?"

"Only because of all their privileges."

"And their meals."

"That's part of their privileges."

"They're like another race," Dib said. "The Master Race."

Dib was munching on some Black Crows. He was always eating. Eating stuff like Hostess Ding Dongs, M&M's, Fruit Bars, and Sno-Caps. Dib was like most kids who'd rather eat Whoppers at Burger King than duckling à l'orange at the best French restaurant. He thought frozen Lean Cuisine was gourmet food, and a box of Sara Lee double chocolate layer cake was a better dessert than fresh-made key lime pie. It wasn't just the food Sevens were privileged to have, that we weren't, that got to Dib. It was the whole aura of Sevens, and it got to everyone. Everyone at Gardner envied them, watched them, gossiped about them, and wished they were part of them.

The night before, Lasher had taken Dib out to Willing Wanda's for Dib's sexual initiation.

When he came back, Dib said, "Did you ever hear an old song called 'Is That All There Is?' "

"Yes. Some woman named Peggy Lee made a record of it. My mom loved it."

"In it, this kid sees a fire and says is that all there is to a fire?"

"Right."

"That's how I felt about what went on at Willing Wanda's."

"You'll feel more when you're in love."

"I hope so. I'd rather eat a box of Mallomars or dig into a plate of Chicken McNuggets."

"Chicken McNuggets," I said, and I put two fingers down my throat and retched.

Dib was working on his paper for the New Boys Competition. There were always rumors about how one got tapped for Sevens, and one of them was that the N.B.C. had something to do with it. All new students were required to write a paper by the last day of October. The theme that year was "They All Chose America." You could choose any group that'd immigrated. Dib was doing the Irish. I got the bright idea to do Japanese-Americans, and to call mine "Arizona Darkness."

I had only the title and some books from the library about President Roosevelt's executive order 9066, which sent 150,000 Japanese Americans to concentration camps back in World War Two. They were given less than forty-eight hours to gather their possessions together for evacuation. Although there were three times as many Americans of Italian descent living on the West Coast, they weren't affected. Neither were German Americans. Only Japanese.

I wanted to answer Delia's letter before I worked on that.

Dib said, "Name some famous Irish-Americans."

"How about the Kennedys?"

"I've got them."

"I want to write a letter before my father gets here," I said, "so don't talk to me, okay?"

"Dear Delia," Dib said, "how are things in Switzerland?"

He thought that's where she was, and that was why I got mail from Switzerland. I let him think it.

Dear Delia [I wrote],

Last week in Classics we read Aeschylus's account
of Clytemnestra's welcoming Agamemnon home from
the Trojan War. She asked him to walk the last few yards
on a purple carpet of great value. He didn't want to do it.
He said it was too valuable to walk on. But she insisted.
Then he went inside the palace and she murdered him in his
bath. . . . I thought of when a girl I loved gave me
a purple bow tie, then stood me up for the Senior Prom. . . .
I got an A + for the paper I wrote about it.

I thought, I'm glad she's in my past. I'm glad there's Delia.

A secret thought. Oscar Wilde once wrote he who
expects nothing will never be disappointed. I don't expect
anything from you, Delia. Will you ever disappoint me?

I'm not sorry about choosing to come to L'Ecole
la Coeur. So far, so good. That night at the Frog Pond?

My back wasn't that sunburned. I wanted to lean into you.

Love, F
    E
      L
        L

I addressed the letter c/o The Worldwide Tours Group, Goodship Cruise, San Francisco, California, for forwarding. Then I put that letter into an envelope addressed to John Fell at L'Ecole la Coeur. Ping would mail it for me.

Just as I was finishing, the buzzer rang three short, one long, my signal.

"Your dad's here," said Dib.

I hadn't seen or talked to Pingree since early September. I never called him, though I'd memorized his phone number in case of emergency. He didn't even want me to write it in my address book. That was just one of his rules, along with others like no photographs of myself at Gardner ever. He said to take sick the day they scheduled class pictures for the yearbook. Avoid all cameras!

I wore the new tan gabardine suit he'd bought me. He had on a dark, vested, pin-striped one.

"What a day!" he said. It was warm and the sun was out. "I'm glad to see you, my boy! I'm glad you're doing so well!"

I walked along beside him, down the path toward chapel.

"I haven't gone below A since I've been here, so it must agree with me. I'm not repeating that much, either. It's harder here than it was in public school."

"Your monthly report was excellent, Fell! That paper you did for classics, what did you call it? The one you got an A+ on?"

" 'The Purple Carpet.' Did they mention that?"

"Dr. Skinner reported that you have a flair for composition. I even showed it to Fern, because of the carpet business. That would be like Ping, you know. He was always intrigued by magic carpets. *The Arabian Nights*. It sounded like Ping."

"It didn't have anything to do with *The Arabian Nights*," I said.

"It doesn't matter. Fern thought it did. She said, 'You see, I was right. He got past all that Tower business.' " Pingree chuckled. He clapped his arm around my shoulder, an inch of ash dropping off his cigarette. "It's working out. You're doing fine!"

"And Ping?"

"He loves it over there! When I spoke to him last night on the telephone, I said, 'Complain a little more. You don't sound like yourself.' "

In chapel, the Gardner choir sang:

> *And youth will still be in our faces*
> *When we cheer for a Gardner crew.*
> *Yes, youth will still be in our faces*
> *We'll remain to Gardner true!*

Pingree wiped tears from his eyes.

After, Pingree said, "I can't stay for Sunday dinner. I don't want to get involved up here, anyway. But good

Lord, it takes me back to walk around this place!"

"How are things in Seaville?"

"The same. Is your mother happy in Brooklyn?"

"They still can't find a decent apartment. But she says it's so good to be a subway ride from Macy's again she doesn't care."

We both chuckled, and then he stopped as he saw The Tower.

"Ah! The Tower!"

"Do you want to walk over there?" I asked him. "My roommate says they're cooking rib roast down in the Sevens's clubhouse for Sunday dinner."

"Yes, their Sunday dinners are always the envy of everyone. Steak Wednesday nights, so they say. The inside of that clubhouse is supposed to be very elegant! No, I'll just admire it from a distance, as I always did."

We started walking along again.

"What did you name your tree?" I asked him.

"My tree. I almost forgot about planting that tree."

"That was one thing you didn't warn me about."

"I completely forgot. You plant it, you forget it. I named mine Sara. That was my first wife's name."

"You knew her way back then?"

"Oh yes. Way back then." He lit another cigarette. "She went to Miss Tyler's in Princeton. You would have liked her. She was always questioning what it all meant. What we were put on this earth for, all that sort of thing. She was a philosophy major. She was my first melancholy baby. Do you know that song?"

"No."

"You don't know 'Melancholy Baby'?"

"No, I don't."

"I can't believe they don't still sing it."

"Maybe they do. I don't know it. I guess Delia's a melancholy baby, too. She doesn't sound like she loves the trip she's on."

"Ah, yes. Delia."

"We write," I said.

"Well, good."

"She's going around the world. Did I tell you that?"

"Yes, you did. Do you really love this Delia, Fell?"

"I don't know."

"That's good, that you don't know."

"Why is it good?"

"Love is such an interference. When it happens to you, you let your guard down. You should never let your guard down."

"I guess you're right," I said. I don't know what he was thinking of, but I was thinking of Keats, and how she'd treated me once she could take me for granted. . . . I still hadn't written to Keats.

"You know, Fell—I should call you Thompson around here, or Tom—I've grown very fond of you."

"Thanks," I said. "I like you, too."

"I'm going to travel next month, and I got worried over the idea what if something happens to me? Where would that leave you? So I've already transferred the first ten thousand to a savings account for you. Here's your book."

"Aren't you afraid I'll skip out on you now that I have the money?" I laughed.

"No. I trust you. I know you won't touch it until your year is over. Your allowance is sufficient, isn't it?"

"Yes, and I have some extra from selling the Dodge."

I took a look at the bank book. It was from the Union Trust Company in Brooklyn Heights. John T. Fell. The T. was for Theodore, my grandfather's name. When I'd gone to the nursing home to tell him that I was going away to school in Switzerland, that I'd won a Brutt scholarship to go there, he'd said, "I was named after Theodore Roosevelt, Johnny. Did I ever tell you why?" I was in a hurry. I had to tell him yes, he'd told me why. I still felt lousy about that.

Pingree said, "I was going to put the money in trust for you, in your mother's name."

"I'm glad you didn't. MasterCard would get their hands on it, or Visa, or some collection agency. My mother owes all over the place."

"I realize that. And you're a big boy. We have to trust each other, don't we, Fell?"

"Yes, we do," I agreed. "I'm working hard on the French, too. By Christmas I'll *sound* like I've been going to L'Ecole la Coeur."

"I'm not worried about you," he said. He let the cigarette drop from his mouth, stepped on it, and said, "Walk me down to my car. I love this place, you know. I was happiest right here."

16

NOVEMBER. I was out in front of Hull House one afternoon reading a letter from Keats. Even if it hadn't been written to me, and wasn't signed, I would have known it was Keats's, right away.

Dear Fell,

Here's a poem I translated for Spanish, written by Pedro Calderon de La Barca (1600–1681).

> *And what is life but frenzy?*
> *And what is it but fancy?*
> *A shadow, mere fiction,*
> *for its greatest good is small,*
> *and life itself a dream,*
> *and dreams are only dreams.*

Doesn't that make you really depressed, Fell? So why am I writing you? It won't help my mood to remember that you caught me out in everything, from going to the prom with Quint to his coming to Four Winds that weekend . . . and

*you never forgave me. I don't blame you. . . . But I was in
Seaville last weekend to see Seaville High play Northport
(I'll always go back for that game). They lost, which was
depressing, too. They only won two games the whole season!*

*Oh, Fell, I'm never going to be supportive of anyone.
I'm always going to need it and never be able to give it,
which makes me practically worthless!*

*One thing I did do when I was home, went to the Stiles
Gallery. Maybe just because I'd heard you dated their
summer au pair and hoped she'd show up there, so I could
get a look at her.*

*Fell, I'm not over you yet, although I gave you every indication
I was. I dream of your smell. The scent awakens me like a
ghost tickling my nose with a thread from its sheet.*

*Also, Mrs. Pingree's work was on display. Early Works,
they were called.* Smiles We Left Behind Us *was there, just
as peculiar as you'd described it, but even more weird was
the painting of seaweed. Just this orange seaweed under
green water. Well, that is not the shock. She called it* Sara.
*It is really strange, Mummy says, because when the first
Mrs. Pingree died (her name was Sara!), there were rumors
Fern Pingree pushed her overboard. She couldn't swim.
She drowned. . . . Seaweed . . . Sara . . . How about that for
weird? It's 10X weirder than anything going on in my life,
which is at a depressing standstill. Is yours?*

*Do you speak French fluently now? I saw L'Ecole la Coeur
advertised in the back of* Town and Country. *Très chic!
Je t'adore! Toujours,*

Keats.

Then from behind me someone shouted, "SEVENS!"

I whirled around. It was Lasher glaring down at me through those thick glasses. I thought of Ping's glasses, and I thought of that suicide back in Brooklyn who my father said wasn't a suicide, because his glasses were smashed beside his body.

I was supposed to answer with seven things that went together.

"Grammar," I said, trying to remember all the seven sciences, "Logic, Arithmetic, Music, Geometry, Astronomy, and . . . and . . ."

"*And?*" Lasher said. "Are you naming the seven medieval sciences?"

"Yes."

"Well, what have you left out?"

"I don't know."

"You left out Rhetoric, Thompson!"

Lasher had on an old tweed topcoat, with the collar up. He had his stubble beard with his stubble mustache. I wished my father'd lived to see stubble get to be an in thing. My father used to come home from all-night jobs unshaved, complaining that he looked like some bum.

"Okay," I said. "The seven names of God. El, Elohim—"

Lasher cut me off. "No second chances, Thompson!"

He came around to face me, his hands sunk in his pockets. The wind blew back his thick black hair. I could never see his eyes. The leaves were off the trees above us. It was a blustery late-fall afternoon. I was cold in just a yellow turtleneck sweater and tan cords.

"I want you to go to The Tower after your dinner tonight," said Lasher, "and place a lighted candle on every step. You'll find the candles and their ceramic holders in a carton outside the Sevens clubhouse. Do you understand, Thompson?"

"What about study hall?"

"Just tell the proctor you're on a Sevens assignment. Get your ass there by seven-thirty. Seven-thirty, sharp, scumbag!"

"All right."

"You go all the way to the top. Then press the clubhouse bell so we can all come out and admire your handiwork before you blow them all out on your way back down."

"All right."

"Stupid!" Lasher growled as he walked away. "You left out Rhetoric!"

It was a Wednesday. We always had a test at the start of French on Thursday mornings. I usually studied hard on Wednesday nights. I wouldn't that Wednesday night. Not after one hundred and twenty steps.

"He's really a sadist," Dib said. "I have a theory about why he is."

"Why is he?"

Dib was eating a Baby Ruth, getting ready for dinner. Our room in Hull House looked as if burglars had just left it. Dib never closed a door he opened, or picked up anything he took off. We never had room inspections. No one ever got on our backs about whether or not the beds were made. The only tyranny at Gardner was Sevens.

"He's mean because God gave him that one flaw," Dib said. "His eyesight. That's the real snake in the grass."

"He ought to get contact lenses. His eyes are real pretty."

"He can't wear them. He gets allergic to anything in his eyes. Creery says if Lasher didn't have to wear those glasses you could shave him, put a dress on him, and ask him to go out on a date."

"Except he wouldn't go out with Creery," I said. "Creery's too much of a stonehead."

"Creery says he's mean because both his parents are shrinks, and shrinks' kids are always messes. Sevens is his real family—that's why he makes so much of it. He's been in Sevens since he was fourteen."

"Maybe he's mean because his family shipped him out when he was so young."

"Or maybe," said Dib, "his family shipped him out when he was so young because he was mean."

The dinner bell rang and we went downstairs and walked across the commons together.

"I'd be a little scared to go up in The Tower by myself after dark," Dib said.

"I'm not looking forward to it."

"You should have packed your gun."

"I never carry it or load it."

"Yeah. Guns scare the hell out of me, too."

"I know a girl who got turned on by the sight of that gun."

"Delia?"

"Yeah, Delia."

"Why don't you have a picture of her?"

"We never took any."

"Ask her for one. I'd like to see this Trembling Delia."

"I've asked her and asked her."

In my last letter to her, I underlined my request in red. When she answered it, she wrote:

Oh, don't tell me you've forgotten how I look, F
E
L
L.

That was all. I shook the envelope to be sure she hadn't put a photograph inside. She hadn't.

I sometimes thought if I hadn't been assigned to Dib for a roommate, I'd walk everywhere alone at Gardner. I wasn't good at making friends with kids whose smiles and clothes and walks shouted money, prep school, connections, tennis!

Dib and I were two of a kind that way. He didn't make friends easily, either. His father wasn't a captain of industry. His father was the great-grandson of one. He drank a lot and raised orchids and a brand of wrinkle-faced dogs called Chinese Shar-Peis. Dib's brother had gone from Gardner to a seminary, to become a priest.

Dib said his mother was strange, too. She went to seances and hunted ducks they raised on their farm for her to hunt.

He'd asked me once if my family was strange. He'd said your father didn't look it, in chapel. What you know about someone from looking at him is zilch, I'd said, but I'd played down my family. I'd just said they were both physicists. I'd said my mother painted.

On the way to dinner that night he asked me how come a physicist had a gun like that?

My one slip. The gun. I'd told Dib my father'd given it to me.

"He's a collector," I said.

"I hope you're not from Mafia," Dib said. "That gun looked like something the Godfather'd pack. Are you sure your real name isn't Pingratti?"

I laughed hard and felt my knees go weak. "No. My real name's not Pingratti," I said.

After dinner I told the proctor I had a Sevens assignment.

"In that case . . ." He shrugged. You could get away with anything at Gardner if Sevens said so.

I walked over to The Tower. The campus lights were on.

I could smell steak. We'd had Spanish rice and beets for dinner.

I could see inside the Sevens clubhouse, where the curtains fell apart in one window near the bottom of the steps.

I looked in.

It was like some kind of movie set in there. MGM filming King Arthur's Court, only the knights were all in light-blue blazers and black top hats. It looked like a convention of chimney sweeps.

There were enough silver candelabras set out on the long dinner table to make Liberace look chintzy. There were four waiters running around in white jackets. I could see floor-to-ceiling bookcases all around the room, and a roaring fire inside a walk-in stone fireplace.

I could see Creery in there with a hand-painted palm tree tie around the neck of one of those formal shirts usually worn under tuxedo jackets. He looked like his old goofy self, the top hat covering his shaved head, two razor-blade earrings dangling from his left earlobe.

I got to work.

I pulled over the carton near the stairs, and began my ascent. I had to drag the carton up with me. There were oven matches inside, and the ceramic holders were tall enough to keep the candles from blowing out in the wind.

I thought about Mom and Jazzy, wishing I could get to Brooklyn for Thanksgiving. I used to always make the stuffing, a corn-bread one with sausage and mushrooms. I longed to cook again. Mom had a job as a hostess in a restaurant down near the World Trade Center in New York City. She was looking for something in catering or fancy food. She'd written that she made just enough money to last the month, unless she bought something. She'd write *Ha! Ha!* after one of her jokes. She'd put it in parentheses. Sometimes she'd write *(Sob!) . . . I miss you (Sob!)*. She said Jazzy was working on costumes for Georgette, since soon Georgette was going to discover her real parents were Rumanian royalty. *(She pronounces it 'Woomanian.' She thinks they dress in furs and crowns.)*

Sometimes in his sleep, Dib would whimper and cry,

"Mommy? Are you there?" He'd get me thinking. Are you there, Mommy? Jazzy? Georgette?

I thought of Delia, too. Delia with the slow smile and long kisses, dancing on the wet grass to "Don't go changing."

I thought of Keats going to the Stiles Gallery, and I thought of a lot of orange seaweed in green water, called *Sara*.

When I was at the top of The Tower, I looked down at all the candles, and I remembered once when the Stileses went out, we'd let the candles burn down in their living room, Delia and I, while we held each other on the long, beige sofa.

It was the first time I'd told her I loved her.

"Don't make me say I love you, Fell."

"Who said you had to say it?"

"I thought you'd expect it because you said it."

"I did, but I'm not going to stay awake nights if you don't say it." I stayed awake a lot of nights because she didn't say it. I knew I would when I said I wasn't going to stay awake nights if she didn't say it.

Just as I was about to go inside the room at the top of The Tower to ring the clubhouse bell, I heard Lasher's voice behind me. I jumped. He held me with his hand around my neck.

"Thompson, look down there at the ground and tell me if it makes you want to jump."

"No, I don't want to jump." My heart was racing. How'd he get up there?

"I named my tree Suicide, Thompson."

"I heard you did. If you want to jump, let go of me first." He held me near the edge of the wall, and I thought, He's crazy. I'm up here by myself with this maniac.

Then Creery's voice came like a sweet release. "Knock it *off*, Lasher!"

Lasher let go of me.

Creery had a lantern flashlight. He was shutting a gate in the little stone-walled room behind us. It was the first time I knew anything about an inside elevator in The Tower.

Creery pushed the clubhouse bell.

It rang out in the windy night. There was a moon overhead, with clouds passing through its face—now you see it, now you don't. Below us, there were shouts as the Sevens poured out of their clubhouse.

Creery put the lantern on the table. He picked up a bullhorn and walked out to where we were.

I thought of sunny days in summer by the ocean when Daddy shouted through his bullhorn, "HELEN? I WANT YOU!"

"SEVENS!" Creery shouted.

Then the Sevens shouted up in thinner voices: "Wisdom! Understanding! Counsel! Power! Knowledge! Righteousness! Godly fear!"

Creery led the singing.

> *The time will come as the years go by,*
> *When my heart will thrill*
> *At the thought of The Hill . . .*

While they sang the song, I remembered something my father'd once said, that anything that is too stupid to be spoken is sung. But it was then that Lasher stopped singing and started talking while they sang, grabbing my shoulders with his hands; behind him, Creery's razor-blade earrings bobbed as he sang and shook his head up and down.

Lasher was calling me Pingree.

"You made Sevens, Pingree!"

Creery said, "Congratulations, Pingree!"

> *And the Sevens who came*
> *With their bold cry,*
> *WELCOME TO SEVENS!*

Lasher and Creery had turned me around so I stood looking down at the candles in the wind, with the moon shifting above us, the sounds of their singing, the lights of Gardner scattered over The Hill.

> *Remember the cry.*
> *WELCOME TO SEVENS!*

Below, with their top hats flying into the night, they shouted seven times: "PINGREE! PINGREE! PINGREE! PINGREE! PINGREE! PINGREE! PINGREE!"

Then Creery said, "We'll take the elevator down to our clubhouse, Pingree."

"Sevens don't walk when they don't have to," Lasher said. Then he smiled at me. "Surprised you, didn't we, Pingree?"

THURSDAY NIGHT at dinner, Gardner's headmaster, J. T. Skinner, announced that the winner of the N.B.C. competition was me . . . for "Arizona Darkness."

I got a handshake and a gold plaque. Then everyone in the dining room stood and applauded.

"You're really stepping in it!" Dib said after lights out.

Well, W. Thompson Pingree was. For sure. It didn't seem like John Fell's luck. My father used to say, "Even in heaven you'll find the wrong people to hang out with, Johnny; you head for trouble like a paper clip toward a magnet." I hoped he was "up there" looking down on me, marveling. I knew I was marveling.

"I'm not trying to find out anything secret about Sevens from you," Dib continued, "but . . ."

"Good! Because I couldn't tell you anything, anyway. I don't have a clue why I got in!"

"But," Dib persisted, "don't you think it's got something to do with the N.B.C. essay?"

"What could it have to do with that? The richest boy

in the whole state of Florida got into Sevens, too, right? His essay didn't even place, didn't even get Honorable Mention." That was true. Monte Kidder was the kid who was dragged out of his bed by the Sevens over in Parker House, some five hours after I got in.

"Right." Dib sounded dejected. "Right. And that guy that sings the solos in chapel, and sounds like a castrato his voice is so high, he got in, too."

"Outerbridge," I said.

"Yeah, Outerbridge."

Outerbridge, Kidder, and Pingree.

We were the only three to make Sevens. We were as different from each other as Sean Penn, Mr. T, and Emmanuel Lewis.

All of us were tapped for Sevens on Wednesday night. All of us were told we'd be initiated into the mysteries of Sevens in seven days, at seven o'clock, in the clubhouse under The Tower.

"It just doesn't add up," Dib said.

"Go to sleep," I said. "I'm going to sleep it off, like it was all a big binge."

That night my brain discarded some neurological junk. I dreamed Lasher pushed me off The Tower and I discovered I could fly. So could Delia. She flapped her arms like slender silver wings, and we glided along in sunny blue skies. "Don't fall!" she called to me, and I saw

F
E
L
L

spelled out as she always wrote my name in letters, going down.

I cabled John Fell the news at L'Ecole la Coeur, and waited for an answer of any kind. Congratulations? Good work, W. Thompson Pingree!? The bonus for Sevens is in the bank, as promised? Something . . . I figured Ping'd find a way to get the news to his father.

Days passed.

Even though I didn't yet know the mysteries of Sevens, I was already basking in its reflected glory. Faculty smiled. J. T. Skinner called out, "Ah! The man of the hour! Hel-lo, there!" Kids whose smiles and clothes and walks shouted money, prep school, connections, tennis, also shouted "Pingree! How're you doing?" Creery gave me a wink, passing me on the commons. Lasher clasped his hands together above his head in a gesture of victory.

In a letter to Delia, I wrote:

I got into a club here that's special, but it makes me melancholy, too, the way champagne tastes flat when you drink it without the one you want there, there. . . . The roses don't smell. The music's too loud. I want to breathe in the smoke of your cigarette, and hear you tell me that you like my French toast. Delia, send a picture. Send a photograph. Send a snapshot. I'll settle for a pencil sketch. I need a fix!

I even wrote to Keats.

You are going at happiness all wrong. Don't go back to your old high school for football games, or into galleries

*featuring orange seaweed called Sara. Don't tell boys
you once stood up you can smell them in your dreams, and
stop translating Spanish poems that say what is life but
frenzy? Don't analyze feelings of worthlessness; there's no
gain in it.*

F

E

L

L

On the weekend, I broke all the rules and called Mom.
I signed out and went down into Cottersville with my
pockets full of change at dinnertime, and found a phone
booth on the corner.

When Jazzy answered, I said, "This is the King of
Rumania. We have reason to believe our little princess
was taken from us years ago by someone at this number."

"Johnny? Where are you?"

"Switzerland, honey! Can't you hear the skiers
swooshing down the mountain right behind me?"

"I wish you was here, Johnny!"

"I wish I were, too, Jazzy!"

"Mommy! Johnny's calling from Switzerland!"

When Mom came on, I said, "I know I'm not supposed to be doing this."

"I'm glad you did, sweetheart!"

"I miss you, Mom. I made Sevens!"

"That snob club?"

"I don't know that it's such a snob club," I said. Oh,

it didn't take much to blow me the other way, did it?

"Johnny! You'll get more money!"

"Yeah! But remember, Mom, money can't buy hap-piness."

"Anyone who says that doesn't know where to shop!"

"I won an essay contest, too, Mom!"

"I'm proud of you, Johnny. . . . Are you happy?"

"I think so. I'm a little confused."

"Me, too. Happy but a little confused. You know how much I owe MasterCard? They just gave me fifteen hundred dollars more credit! I'm going to buy you some-thing to celebrate all your good news!"

"Nothing to wear, Mom, *please*," I said.

When I hung up, the lights were bright up on The Hill. The little town of Cottersville was pretty dead. I walked around until I found a soda shop that had an hour to go before closing. I parked myself at the counter and ordered a Western on toast with mustard, and a vanilla soda without ice cream. I longed for the old egg creams I used to buy in Brooklyn. The soda wasn't even close.

I saw a copy of *The Cottersville Compass* on a rack by the door, and bought myself a copy for fifty cents.

I turned the pages slowly while I ate, and came to my own photograph on page six. I was shaking hands with Dr. Skinner, the night he gave me the gold plaque.

I hadn't even been aware of a camera in the dining room, but someone had been there with one, because there I was in all my glory, smiling up at the headmaster in my Brooks Brothers navy blazer with the gray pants.

Under my photograph was

W. Thompson Pingree wins essay contest for new boys.

Under that was my essay.

ARIZONA DARKNESS

Picture rows of tar-papered buildings surrounded by barbed wire fences, set down in an empty wasteland blown by swirling dust and whistling winds. . . .

I remembered Pingree's saying to me, "Don't *ever* let anyone take your picture!"

I began to panic. The picture. The essay. And her title: *Arizona Darkness.*

The Cottersville Compass was only a weekly with a small circulation, but I knew from so many of my father's cases how things could begin to unravel through little slips.

I decided to do something risky. I'd call Fernwood Manor, hoping Pingree would answer. If *she* answered, I'd hang up and try to think of another tack. But if he answered, I'd just say, "I need to talk to you! Can you call me tonight in an hour or so?"

I got more change from the girl behind the counter. I recognized Billy Joel's voice singing on the radio and it made me think of Delia. I wished that summer had never ended.

I left half the toasted Western behind. There was too much mustard on it, anyway. I put a few bills down to cover my check, and went back out into the street to find the phone booth again.

I dialed 516, then Pingree's number, which I knew by heart, and put in a lot of change when the operator told me the charges.

I got an answering machine.

It was Fern Pingree's voice.

"You've reached 555-2455. We are not able to answer the phone just now. At the sound of the beep, please leave your message. If this is you, Woody, there's an emergency. Come here or call the Institute. Woody, if this is you, there's an emergency."

18

FOUR DAYS WENT BY. Still no word from Pingree. Nothing from John Fell in Switzerland, either.

I knew Pingree was planning to travel in late November. He'd told me that when he'd presented me with the bank book. But it was only the second week in the month. I couldn't figure out what kind of an emergency would prompt his wife to leave that message on the phone answering machine, or why she wouldn't know where he was.

I made myself stop thinking about it. There were too many projects to finish before Christmas vacation. I had a paper due on the cosmological theory of the big bang, for science. I had to finish an analysis of Euripedes' plays for classics. For French, we were supposed to compose a Christmas poem called "La Paix." There was a major Latin test scheduled for the first week in December.

Then there was the move from Hull House into

Sevens House, which was to be completed before the Sevens's dinner.

I'd finished that late Wednesday afternoon, with Dib's help.

I asked Dib to walk partway to The Tower with me that night. After I left the Sevens's clubhouse, at the end of the dinner, I'd be going straight over to Sevens House. I'd be a bona fide member then, an object of awe and envy for the rest of my days at Gardner.

"You look a little down for someone who's lucked out all over the place," Dib said.

"Did you see anyone with a camera at the N.B.C. dinner?"

"Just Mr. Parish, Gardner's P.R. man. Why?"

"I wonder if he'll take pictures at this dinner?"

"Nobody goes inside that clubhouse but Sevens members and the help. Is that all you've got to worry about now, whether someone's going to get your shining hour on film?"

"I don't want my shining hour on film."

"No, not much. I never saw anyone primp the way you just did."

I'd showered, shaved, cut my nails, cleaned under what was left, and refrained from dousing myself with Aramis. I'd remembered what Cadman, the owner of Plain and Fancy, used to say about wearing cologne or after-shave to sit-down dinners. Don't. It ruined the smell of the food.

It was raining out, wanting to snow. Dib was holding the umbrella. He was in the oldest clothes he could find.

I was in rust cotton trousers with a thin navy stripe, the navy blazer, a white shirt, a polka dot tie, and just-shined black loafers.

I slung one arm around Dib's shoulders. "This isn't going to change that much between us. We're still going to see a lot of each other, Dib."

"Sure. In classes. Study hall."

"Movies. We'll go to movies."

"They've got a VCR in Sevens House with a screen the size of the side of a house."

"I'm not going to get stuck up, Dib."

"You say now."

"I'll say later, too."

"Later we'll see what you say."

I stopped him halfway along the commons.

"I don't want you to go the rest of the way with me."

"I understand," he said, as though the reason were him.

"I just don't want the Sevens to think I brought some-one along for courage."

"You did," Dib said.

"Yeah, but they don't have to know I did."

I gave his arm a light punch. "Okay, scumbag, from now on stay out of my way."

"Very funny," he said sadly. He wasn't taking it well. I was. I didn't like moving out on him, but I was champ-ing at the bit to hear about the mysteries, get a good meal, and go directly to Boardwalk . . . or heaven . . . or whatever you wanted to nickname Sevens House. The beds over there were bigger and firmer than those in

Hull House. There were thick rugs on the floors, fireplaces in some of the rooms; only two shared a bathroom. Lights out was when you wanted lights out, and your room was cleaned, your bed made, by a maid.

"Okay, Dibble," I said. "I'll be around, pal."

"Me, too, Thompson. Don't you want the umbrella? I don't need it in these clothes."

"I don't want to look all fresh like the blushing bride," I said. "A little wet'll be good."

But it was starting to come down hard and cold. I ran the rest of the way to The Tower.

Lionel Schwartz presided over the dinner that night in the Sevens clubhouse.

He was known around campus as the Lion. He was in all the school plays, a good-looking senior, the type who wore bow ties and leather patches on his sports coat, and had permission from home to smoke a pipe he could never keep lit.

The room was filled with candles; even the chandelier above our heads held candles. The Sevens seemed to be candle freaks. They all had on their top hats and their light-blue blazers with the 7's on the pockets. There was a fire going. Creery sat across from me, grinning at me.

We were served filet mignon, baked potato with sour cream, fresh green beans, salad, and hot rolls.

Creery said, "Over in the dining room, this would be a menu for an alumni banquet, or for the boys who don't get to go home for Christmas. We eat like this all the time here."

I smiled, but I felt my first pang of guilt at being among

the elite. I wondered how I'd gotten in—and if I could stick it out.

They even served artichoke curries to Lasher and Outerbridge, the two vegetarians.

We all gulped down dinner and sat waiting for dessert.

Schwartz banged his fork against a crystal goblet for silence, then stood up and began: "There are seven days in creation, seven days in the week, seven graces, seven divisions in the Lord's Prayer, and seven ages in the life of man."

"SEVENS!" the old members chorused.

The three of us—Outerbridge, Kidder, and I—looked at each other questioningly, trying to figure out what we had in common.

I was sure I saw Kidder's lip curl with distaste at the thought that we had anything in common. He thought he was Mel Gibson. He almost was, take away ten or twelve years. He had his own red Mercedes. He'd had a date once with Molly Ringwald, and her photograph was on his desk. He began sentences, "It's my sense that . . ." or "Correct me if I'm wrong, but . . ." as though he were addressing a committee. They said Kidder had a boat, as long as the front of Saks Fifth Avenue, moored in Key West.

And Outerbridge? Not nearly as charismatic. More asthmatic. Known for his beautiful sister, Cynthia, a Bryn Mawr freshman. He was a vegetarian. A near soprano who excelled at singing hymns such as "Lead, Kindly Light" in chapel. A redhead. A mad, crazy giggler in movies, the type you turned around to stare and hiss at, because he laughed through the next lines of the joke.

Schwartz looked down the long table toward us. "What I'm going to tell you now, no Sevens has ever told an outsider. You are on your honor *never* to reveal the reason for your selection in Sevens! Repeat after me: So be it, solemnly sworn!"

"So be it," we three said, "solemnly sworn."

"It is in the highest tradition of Gardner," said Schwartz, "that you did nothing to earn this distinction, that nothing you *are* earned it for you, that nothing your family is secured this high honor for you!

"Gardner has never stressed background over accomplishment, physical appearance over mental prowess, anything over anything, or anyone over anyone. We are all equal, and yet . . ."

Schwartz paused for a long few seconds.

"And yet . . ." he paused again, and looked hard at us: Outerbridge, Kidder, and me. "Gardner would be remiss not to point out one great lesson in life. Gardner prepares you for life, and in preparing you, points out that you are never truly prepared. For an unexpected circumstance can change your fortune . . . *pffft*"—a brush of his fingers through the air—"like that! Chance is something out of your control!"

Then all the old members said softly, "Mere chance."

"Mere chance made you all Sevens," said Schwartz. "Sevens will make you more, but you did nothing for the privilege. You three new members were chosen as we old ones were, because you named the trees you planted your first day here with seven-letter words.

"Kidder named his Key West. Outerbridge named his Cynthia. And Pingree named his Good-bye. There are seven letters in Gardner, too.

"It is no more complicated than that. . . . It is as whimsical as the fickle finger of Fate. But from this moment on, you are privileged. You can never be expelled from Gardner for any reason! You will always have special privileges! Gardner will become a different experience for you than it is for the others.

"*And*"—another long pause—"when you leave Gardner, you will connect with a national, and in some cases an international, fraternity of Sevens alumni that will help you throughout your life!"

You could hear a pin drop in that room while the three of us took this in.

Then Schwartz said, "Only another Sevens knows that you are here by . . ."

"Mere chance," the old members said.

"And so," Schwartz said, "you have been given a favor by mere chance. Sevens hopes you will accept it with grace, gladness of heart, and thanks to God!"

The old members began to sing:

> *When I was a beggar boy,*
> *And lived in a cellar damp,*
> *I had not a friend or a toy,*
> *But that was all changed by mere chance!*

Once I could not sleep in the cold,
And patches they covered my pants,
Now I have bags full of gold,
For that was all changed by mere chance!
Mere chance, mere chance,
Mere chance makes us gay,
Mere chance makes night day,
But whoever she'll choose,
She can also make lose,
Mere chance has her way,
Mere chance!

They ended with a thunderous "WELCOME TO SEVENS!"

From the ceiling, a square-shaped, enormous silver tray descended slowly. On it were three top hats and three light-blue blazers with three white carnations in the buttonholes.

Through the door from the kitchen, waiters came carrying flaming Cherries Jubilee on silver platters.

I walked slowly back toward Sevens House in a misty rain after. I'd hung back a little so I could walk alone. I felt good. I kept thinking of Pingree's saying, "I was happiest right here." I wasn't happiest, but I *was* happy.

What I liked best about getting into Sevens was that it was really just a fluke. I'd almost called my tree Adieu, which would have meant I'd have missed by two letters.

Schwartz had named his tree after the rock star Madonna, and another guy had called his Cormier, after the man who wrote *The Chocolate War*.

I could live with the reason I'd gotten into Sevens.

◻

When I got inside Sevens House, the housemother came gliding across to me in a velvet robe that touched the floor, the same color as her blond hair, which was held back in a bun. She looked like some model out of a fashion ad, about to ask me to share the fantasy.

"Are you Woodrow Pingree, Jr., dear?"

"Yes. Only I call myself W. Thompson Pingree. Thompson, or Tom, for short. And you're?"

Not a day over thirty. Oh, I would confide all my troubles to this one. I would tell her about a Spanish poet who said life was itself a dream, and dreams are only dreams.

"I'm Mrs. Violet. I'm glad I caught you."

"I'm easy to catch, Mrs. Violet."

"You're not, though. I've been waiting and waiting for you, dear. Your mother is here."

"My what?"

"Your mother."

"Not mine."

"Mrs. Pingree. Yes. She's right outside in that big, long white limousine."

"She is?"

"I was hoping she'd see you come in."

"I came up the side path. My *mother*? Mrs. Fern Pingree?"

My heart was hammering under my shirt. I figured Mrs. Violet could see my blazer move in and out.

I looked out the front door and saw a white stretch limo.

"What a beautiful car!" said Mrs. Violet. And with a gentle push at my shoulders, she added, "You'd better hurry, dear. She's been waiting a long time. She wouldn't wait in our little reception area."

So I went back out into the misty, cold night and walked very slowly down toward the Cadillac.

The back door opened as I approached.

Fern Pingree sat forward in a fur over her shoulders, a white turtleneck sweater, and black leather pants, her small, almond-shaped eyes suddenly very large.

"You!" she said.

I tried to think of what to say. I bent down, peering into the backseat, when hands grabbed me.

They were not her hands.

A man I'd never seen before introduced himself by pulling me the rest of the way inside, holding me by the throat.

He reached back and shut the car door.

"No!" Mrs. Pingree said. "This isn't Ping!"

"This isn't your son?" said the man.

"This is John Fell," she said. "Let go of him. We're not taking him. Where's Ping, Fell?"

"Your son," I managed to choke out, "is in Switzerland." My neck felt as if it'd been in a vise. I moved from my knees to the small jump seat facing Mrs. Pingree and her henchman.

The driver said, "What do we do now?" He didn't bother to turn around when he spoke.

"Where's Woodrow Pingree? Ask him," the henchman said.

"I think I know where Woody is," said Mrs. Pingree. "I think he's also in Switzerland. Right, Fell?"

"I don't know where your husband is."

"Who is this kid?" the driver said.

"It doesn't matter to you," said Mrs. Pingree. "He's no use to us. Both the fish and the bait are in Switzerland. Right, Fell?"

"Ping is," I said. I could smell the sweet gardenia perfume she wore.

"Yes, I'm beginning to get it now. Ping is at L'Ecole la Coeur. He's there as you, and you're here as Ping. Is that how it worked?"

"I'm here as Ping," I admitted.

"And you last saw my husband when?"

"About a month ago."

"Yes," she said. "He went to Atlantic City about a month ago. He must have come here then."

The henchman said, "What do we do now?"

"We say good night to John Fell," said Mrs. Pingree. "Let him out!"

from *The New York Times*:

BRUTT PHYSICISTS NAMED AS SPIES

Spy Ring Tipped by Chinese Defector

SAN FRANCISCO—Woodrow Thompson Pingree, Sr., 58, surrendered to Federal agents here late yesterday, and was charged with passing United States intelligence secrets to the People's Republic of China.

Clued to the fact the Federal Bureau of Investigation was shadowing and wiretapping him and his wife, Fern, 37, as they plied their trade, Mr. Pingree was reported to be about to flee to Switzerland.

Fern Pingree, still being sought by authorities, is the alleged ringleader of an espionage coterie that passed classified documents for nearly nine years to the Chinese. She is said to have recruited Mr. Pingree sometime after their marriage, while they were both employed at the Brutt

Institute in Bellhaven, New York. There, both Pingrees were privy to highly sensitive nuclear research and had top security clearances.

Unbeknownst to Mrs. Pingree, her husband had enrolled his son by a former marriage, Woodrow Thompson Pingree, Jr., 16, in L'Ecole la Coeur, in Switzerland, under a false name, apparently to put him out of harm's way, and Mrs. Pingree's reach, while he made preparations to leave the country. Apparently long reluctant to continue in the espionage work his wife was committed to, in the last six months Mr. Pingree was liquidating his holdings and disentangling himself from debts incurred by gambling.

The defection last month of Wu Chu-Teng, 63, a double agent from the People's Republic of China, was said to have precipitated the investigation of the Pingrees.

"Come in, Thompson," said J. T. Skinner. "Shut the door after you. There's no point in calling you that anymore. What do you prefer to be called?"

"Fell."

"Of course. By your last name, as all Sevens are called."

The headmaster of Gardner was a lot like his office: big, friendly-looking, immaculate. He even had a manicure. He had a large belly, covered by a vest with brown-and-white checks, and a gold Phi Beta Kappa key. He had on one of those unpressed tweed suits that made him look relaxed and slightly English. He was bald and gray eyed, with a ruddy complexion.

He sat back in a leather swivel chair behind his mahogany desk and pointed to the straight-backed chair in front of his desk. I sat down in it.

Behind him, through his office window, I could see snow coming down from the late-afternoon sky.

"Well, Fell, I've talked with the FBI agents, as you have. We'd better have *our* talk now that some of the smoke has cleared away. You'd better thank your lucky stars that you made Sevens."

"Yes, sir."

"I'm a legacy, you know. When I came to The Hill as a boy, it was my dream to make Sevens. My father was a Sevens."

"I didn't know that, sir."

"He told me not to count on it, and not to think there was anything wrong with me if I didn't make it, but I was still very disappointed. You know how a boy feels—that he can't measure up to his old man."

"Yes, sir."

"If you hadn't made Sevens, you'd be a very disappointed young man, too—assuming that you like it here. Do you?"

"Yes, I do, sir."

"You'd be held reprehensible for enrolling at Gardner under a false identity. I'd probably have to expel you. I can't expel a Sevens. *You* made it. Young Pingree didn't. So you're under the protection of Sevens. Of course, I could ask you to resign."

"Are you, sir?"

"No, I'm not, Fell."

I watched the snow come down behind him.

He said, "Of course, if the Sevens didn't want you among them, they could make it very uncomfortable for you. There was a case like that a few years back. There was a Sevens member suspected of dealing cocaine. While he was under investigation we couldn't touch him, even though we knew he was guilty. Sevens gave him an immunity from immediate disciplinary measures. But the Sevens made life so unbearable for him that he re-signed. That won't happen to you, according to Schwartz. The boys are behind you."

"I'm glad to hear that, sir."

"You have a good record. You won the N.B.C. com-petition, too. . . . I'm a little curious about that, Fell. I know you're probably tired by now of being questioned, but did the infamous Fern Pingree coach you about life in a Japanese internment camp?"

"No, she didn't, sir. I hardly knew her."

"The newspapers say her grandfather died at Jerome, in Arizona, back in World War Two."

"I didn't see that article. I only saw the write-up in *The Times*."

"I'll give you what I've got there on my desk, if you're interested. There's a lot more being written about her now in *Time*, *Newsweek*, and the tabloids."

"I'd like to look at it."

"They still haven't found her."

"I should think she'd have been easy to find in that white stretch Caddy she showed up here in."

"She rented that in Philadelphia. That's where they

lost her trail. Oh, they'll find her," he said. "I was just curious what you know about her."

"No more than I told the FBI agents," I said. I'd been grilled by them for hours on the morning after Mrs. Pingree had made her attempt to kidnap Ping. They'd explained that if she'd gotten Ping, Pingree would have kept his mouth shut about anything to do with the espionage operation at Brutt. Now he'd probably cooperate in exchange for immunity or a lighter sentence.

"And Woodrow Pingree," said Dr. Skinner, picking up a gold letter opener to pass from hand to hand while he talked, "what did you think of him?"

"I liked him, sir. It's impossible for me to believe he sold secrets to China. I didn't even know he was a gambler."

"All around he's not casting the best light on Gardner," Skinner said with an ironic chuckle.

"He always said he was happiest here."

"I have no doubt, considering what came later. I looked him up in his yearbook. Want to see?"

He passed across the light blue leather-bound book with THE HILL BOOK, 1944 stamped across it in white.

There was a rubber band holding back page 23.

There was a photograph of this dark-haired kid with a faint smile on his face and bright, earnest eyes.

WOODROW THOMPSON PINGREE
Sewickley, Pennsylvania
"Woody"
First Prize Westinghouse Science Talent Search '43; Student
Council '43; Captain, Baseball '43; Secretary, Current Events

Club '43; Upper School Tennis Champion—Singles '43; Highest
Average in Form '44; Cum Laude '43, '44; Upper School Tennis
Champion—Doubles '44; Science Club President '44; Senior House
Prefect '44; Choir '43, '44.
Ambition: To be a good Marine.
Remembered For: Ask Sara!
Slogan: Semper Fidelis!
Future Occupation: Move over, Einstein!

I gave the book back to Skinner.

"You just never know, do you?" Skinner said.

"I think *she* did it to him."

"Nobody does it to you, Fell. You do it to yourself.
You have choices. You make your own choices."

"But he was under her spell. Even the papers said
she recruited him."

"According to the tabloids, he wasn't under her spell
recently." He'd picked up the letter opener again and
was playing with it as he talked. "What's the real Ping
like?"

"He's interested in magic. He didn't like her, either.
There were some rumors that she was responsible for
his mother's death."

"I read about that. They were out in a boat together
when the first Mrs. Pingree was drowned."

"Where did you read that?"

"It's all in these magazines and papers. Here, take
them with you." He leaned forward in his swivel chair
and picked them off a pile on his desk. They were all
open to the pages with the write-ups on the Pingrees.
As he passed them across to me I caught glimpses of

Fernwood Manor, Pingree with his arm around Fern Pingree, and one of Pingree with Ping.

I could pick out random sentences:

. . . They never lived ostentatiously—Fern Pingree bought her wardrobe off the rack. . . .

. . . She was an old-school spy, doing it out of conviction, long embittered by old memories of her Japanese grandfather's World War II internment, by Hiroshima, and by a belief that the United States was anti-Asian in its Vietnam policies, as well. . . .

. . . He was her opposite, the modern spy, convictionless, and only in it for the reported $300,000 paid them over the years, a gambler with vast real estate holdings on Long Island, in Atlantic City, and Nevada, and . . .

Dr. Skinner said, "You'll have time to look at all of that later, Fell."

It was hard for me to stop thumbing through what was on my lap.

"Are the other boys treating you well, Fell?" Skinner asked.

"Very well. They're just full of questions."

. . . reports of a romantic involvement that was also said to have prompted Pingree's withdrawal from his wife's espionage . . .

"You'd be wise to tell the other boys you can't talk about the matter, Fell, and be sure not to talk to any reporters. This isn't the kind of publicity Gardner seeks."

"I realize that, sir. I'll be careful."

"Another thing, Fell. You can't continue as a junior. You'll have to be entered as a senior and make up any back work on your own time."

"Yes, sir."

I'd shifted in the chair so I could turn the copy of *Time* around and see what was on the next page.

That was when I saw her.

"You'll have a lot of homework ahead on your Christmas vacation," said Skinner.

It was Delia, in a raincoat, with a scarf around her long black hair, a cigarette going in one hand, a large satchel over the other arm.

> Delia Tremble, 25, questioned in Zurich about her relationship to Pingree, says, "I'll stand by him forever."

"So far," Skinner said, "you haven't made the news, but I suppose they'll get around to it."

"I suppose so," I said.

> . . . began two years ago when the pair met in Atlantic City, where Pingree went to gamble. Miss Tremble denies knowing anything about the Brutt operation, but admits she was helping Pingree escape.

"EVERYONE IN MY FAMILY'S so strange—I didn't pay much attention to your strangeness. That's how you got away with it," Dib said.

"My strangeness?"

"The gun. I would have thought harder about the gun."

"And what else?"

"Your interest in cooking. Remember, once I asked you who taught you to cook, and you said your mother. Then in another conversation, you said you'd worked in a gourmet shop and gotten your interest in cooking there."

"No one's perfect. But I'm not so different now, am I?"

"You're more popular. First Sevens, then this. You've become a star at The Hill."

"The public is fickle, though, Dib. After Christmas I'll be the senior who can't keep up with his class."

We were on the bus to Trenton, New Jersey. I had a wire from Keats in my pocket.

> MUST SEE YOU HOPE YOU CAN COME TO
> ADIEU OVER HOLIDAYS ALL IS FORGIVEN
> DADDY SAYS OR I'LL DRIVE INTO BROOKLYN
> DID I SAY I'D ACTUALLY GO TO BROOKLYN OH
> FELL ONLY YOU CAN LIFT ME FROM MY DE-
> PRESSING DOLDRUMS AND YES I WANT TO HEAR
> ALL ABOUT THE MYSTERIOUS DELIA WILL YOU
> TELL ME THINE UNTIL DEATH KEATS

"Anyway," Dib said, "you're not a star in Lasher's eyes, are you?"

"No, not in his." I'd heard he was the only Sevens who voted for my resignation.

"Creery says he calls you Felon behind your back."

"And to my face."

"Maybe he'll lay off Creery for a while and concentrate on you. The new snake in the grass."

"Probably."

"By the way, I overheard a knockdown fight between them while all this upheaval was going on. I'd gone over to Sevens House looking for you. . . . Lasher was accusing Creery of getting help getting into Sevens." Dib looked over at me to get my reaction. "Can you get help?"

"I'm not going to talk about Sevens."

"Lasher shouted at Creery, 'Your father helped you and his helped him!' "

"I don't know anything about it," I said. But I'd wondered about something like that. If Pingree'd been a

Sevens, for example, and if Ping had gone to Gardner, would Pingree have told Ping about choosing a seven-letter word for his tree . . . or would he have been honorable and not told him? And I laughed to myself. *Honorable*. Pingree . . . That was like saying *Hot*. Snow.

"Sorry I mentioned it," said Dib, "but your name came up, too."

"How did I get into it?"

"Lasher said, 'You and Pingree don't belong in Sevens! Neither of you got in honestly!' Then it sounded like they were knocking each other around the room, and Lasher was shouting, 'I'll kill you!' I made tracks at that point, scared they'd spill out into the hall."

"Yeah," I said. "He's going to have it in for me. That's the least of my worries right now."

"Fell?" Dib said. "Listen, I never said I was sorry about Delia."

"You didn't have to."

"I didn't know if you wanted to talk about it."

"I didn't. Still don't." I never will want to talk about it, I thought. I'll never be able to talk about it.

"Okay with me," Dib said.

He looked out the window. The farm country was disappearing and the tacky suburbs of Trenton were coming into view. I'd get the train to New York City after we got off the bus.

"But thanks, Dib."

My first night home I made spaghetti alla carbonara for Mom and Jazzy. Georgette was dressed in a long black gown with a gold crown on her head, in my honor. Jazzy had propped her up against a corn flakes box in the kitchen. There was a royal-blue ribbon across her gown saying WELCOME HOME, JOHNNY!

Jazzy was in watching TV while I fried the bacon to go into the spaghetti.

I knew Mom'd been wanting to say something she didn't want Jazzy to hear. I thought it might have to do with Delia.

"There's something on my mind, Johnny."

"I know."

"Do you know what it is?"

"Is it her? Because I don't feel like talking about her yet, Mom."

"No, it isn't about her. You'll have to work that out yourself. It's about the money. It's about the ten thousand dollars Mr. Pingree put in the bank for you."

"What about it? Do you need it to get out of hock?"

"I don't appreciate that crack, Johnny."

"I'm sorry, Mom. I didn't mean to put it so crudely. Do you need it?"

"No, I don't need it. And you don't need it, either."

I dropped some onions in with the bacon.

"I was wondering about that," I said.

"There's nothing to wonder about. I don't care that the money was left in the grandfather's will—if that story's even true. We've had too much to do already with those people and their money. I think any money that comes from them is bad money! Your father would roll over in his grave, Johnny! They sold our country's secrets to the enemy! Your father fought for this country! He loved this country!"

"I know."

"You can't help the fact your tuition was paid by that man, and you have to go back and graduate. But we don't want that ten thousand dollars!"

"What'll we do with it?"

"Give it to some good cause."

"I'm not a good cause?"

"You know what I mean, Johnny. Your father used to get tears in his eyes when anyone sang 'The Star-Spangled Banner.' "

"Maybe because he couldn't ever remember the words. He'd get as far as 'Oh, say can you see, by the dawn's early light'—then stop cold."

"Can you go any further?"

"Not really."

"Then don't talk, Big Mouth!"

I turned on the heat under the water for the pasta.

Mom said, "I thought you might give me a fight."

"I never won one with you yet."

"We'll figure out something to do with the money."

"Okay."

"Are you planning to see Keats?"

"Probably."

"I knew you'd give in."

"I'm not giving in. She's going to come all the way to Brooklyn."

"Big deal! She doesn't deserve Brooklyn! Brooklyn's too good for her!"

I said, "Tell Jazzy dinner in ten minutes."

"Is that what they teach you at that fancy school? To order your mother around?"

"Please," I added.

"Johnny," she said, "there are nice girls in this world, honey. I don't want you to lose sight of that. Keats and that other one—they're the exceptions. I know you've been hurt but . . ."

"Not by Keats," I said. My damn voice cracked. I couldn't have gone on, anyway. I still couldn't even get Delia's name out. I didn't want Mom to see my eyes start to fill, so I ducked my head around the corner into the living room. I shouted, "Jazzy? Georgette's being whisked away by bandits!"

"Get their license numbers!" Jazzy yelled back.

The next day, I walked down to Carroll Gardens to visit my grandfather in the nursing home.

"I was named after Theodore Roosevelt," he said when he saw me walk into the room. "Did I ever tell you why?"

"Tell me again," I said. I gave him a kiss and sat down in the chair beside his bed.

"Well, it's a long story," he began.

"Take your time," I said.

So that was how I spent my Christmas vacation. Like my father used to say, "You got your family. You got your health. You got Brooklyn. What else do you need?"

What is there to say about Delia?

From the time she first walked into Plain and Fancy to the time she wrote me letters saying things like Tell me if you think you made the right decision going to Switzerland, she was keeping an eye on me for Pingree.

I remembered so many things: the phone call Pingree made that first night I ran into the Mitsubishi, when he said to somebody that he wouldn't be by, that something had come up. The time we'd all gone back to our house after dinner at Lunch, when he kept encouraging me to keep my date with Delia. I remembered him telling me he liked cards, too, but not card tricks: He liked to play cards. And Delia telling me how her life had changed after the gamblers took over her hometown, Atlantic City.

Pingree'd arranged everything, from her job as au pair at the Stileses' to the cruise she went on until he warned her that he was turning himself in. Then she flew to Zurich to be with Ping.

I don't know what Delia knew about Pingree's double life, or even if she knew that he had one.

I don't even know if there really was something in his father's will about money for Ping when he graduated from Gardner, and more money if he made Sevens. I somehow think that all of that was true, but as my mother's fond of pointing out: The man's a liar.

All I really know for sure is that Pingree was planning to leave the country and begin a new life with Delia and Ping. Then a double agent named Wu Chu-Teng changed all that.

Fern Pingree was arrested three days before Christmas in New York City. I saw a picture of her in the paper, with those white-framed dark glasses on, being escorted by two FBI men. She had no comment.

◻

Sometimes I still hear Fern Pingree saying, "Dreams are the trash bag of the brain!" But that hasn't stopped me from going over and over certain dreams. Because I still dream of Delia. She's flying with me through blue summer skies, dancing with me on wet grass, her eyes watching mine the way they used to. And she's telling me again not to make her say she loves me. She never did say that, awake or dreaming.

◻

About two weeks after I returned to Gardner, one cold Wednesday afternoon, there was a crowd gathered down by The Tower. I jogged that way to see what all the excitement was about. There were snowdrifts all around. We'd hit a record for bad weather in January.

"Fell! Hurry, Fell!" Dib shouted at me.

I pushed my way toward him, and before I got to the front of the crowd, Dib said, "It's Lasher! He jumped from the top!"

Someone else said, "He finally did it!"

Dib turned and told me, "He's committed suicide, Fell!"

I stood there beside Dib, looking down at the cold pavement.

Beside Lasher's body, I saw his thick glasses with the panes smashed.

Then, in less time than it takes a paper clip to inch over to a magnet, I said, "No. He didn't kill himself."

Those five words were going to get me into a lot of trouble.

Someday I'll tell you about it.

ABOUT THE AUTHOR

M. E. Kerr is the winner of the 1993 Margaret A. Edwards Award for her lifetime achievement in writing books for young adults. In announcing the award the ALA Young Adult Library Services Association cited M. E. Kerr for being "one of the pioneers in realistic fiction for teenagers. Her courage to be different and to address touchy current issues without compromising, but with a touch of leavening humor, has earned her a place in young adult literature and in the hearts of teenagers."

M. E. Kerr was born in Auburn, New York, attended the University of Missouri, and now lives in East Hampton, New York.